HAUNTS

HAUNTS

a novel

JOHN DOUGLAS

...

ST. MARTIN'S PRESS
New York

Library of Congress Cataloging-in-Publication Data

Douglas, John.
    Haunts / John Douglas.
        p.   cm.
    ISBN 0-312-05097-6
    I. Title.
    PS3554.O8257H38   1990
    813'.54—dc20

                                                    90-36139
                                                       CIP

First Edition: September 1990

10 9 8 7 6 5 4 3 2 1

for Dad

HAUNTS

··· 1 ···

Even after two or three days of downpour in the mountains, the flood still caught everyone off guard.

The West Virginia small towns were clobbered first—Marlinton on the Greenbrier River, Parsons on the Cheat, Moorefield on the South Branch. Name the town in the region, and it saw devastation. Name the river, and it was crazily over its head those terrible November days.

Trailers floated off their foundations and bobbed in the swirling brown water like toy ships in a bathtub. No plumber could turn off the faucets or cut the power to the pump. The water rose until it poured over the tub and rushed full blast across the flat floodplain.

Farmers hurried to move tractors and expensive equipment to high ground. Their pickup trucks were loaded heavy with whatever would fit, but there just wasn't enough warning, wasn't enough time.

They turned the livestock loose to fend for themselves, but even at that, a drowned milk cow, her udder bulging, was found hanging as if lynched from the supports of a Cheat River bridge two days later.

At the height of the massacre, a dog sped down the Potomac, the poor mutt on its raft of a roof, barking in fright as it tugged at the chain linking it to its doghouse.

Monday night, a young couple abandoned their car on a flooded road near Petersburg and ran inside an empty house to get away from the storm. As the water reached into the second floor, they climbed out onto the roof. Still not good enough. The old dwelling shifted and lifted and splintered into pieces. The man clutched a sycamore for hours until he was finally saved. His wife was hurled downstream and never found.

In the Eastern Panhandle, riverbank cabins belonging to weekenders from Washington and Baltimore left their posts and crashed against each other in the water. One sailed down the Cacapon River until it rammed into a railroad bridge, fitting as neat as a hard rubber stopper into the stone arch, blocking the normal water path, forcing the angered river up over the bridge, up over the tracks, and the trains stopped running.

Paw Paw's downtown was river bottom on Tuesday night. From the highway, you couldn't see the Potomac River bridge any longer. Everyone assumed it had washed out like countless others, but when the sun came up on a gloomy Wednesday, the bridge still stood, its yellow safety light bravely blinking.

At Hancock, on the Maryland banks, the Potomac crested early Wednesday morning, just about the time rescuers helped a stranded woman from her second-story window into a motorboat that navigated Main Street.

Even Shawnee, where flood control walls had been built in the 1950s, wasn't completely spared, though it certainly could have been worse. The tall concrete walls protected the business district. They just couldn't save everything in the lower end of Shantytown, near the old canal.

• • •

Harter could remember standing with his father at the West Side bridge, watching the work crews put in the massive flood control project where the creek—*the crick,* as his father had said it—where the creek emptied into the main river.

Early 1950s, and the powers-that-be had promised nothing like '36 would ever come again. Man had learned to control nature, they'd believed. The ones who'd preached such a rosy sermon were the same guys who'd lectured about a future with safe, cheap nuclear power where we'd all be rich and healthy and jet about in flying cars.

Now it was thirty years later, 1985, Harter was forty-three, and they still spouted off about Progress, capital P. Now they claimed tourist dollars would resurrect Shawnee, which had been fighting for a decade to keep the lid off the coffin as, one by one, the factories shut down.

Christ. Liz would say he was getting cynical. Maybe he was. Or maybe he was only tired. This morning he felt like he was the canal towpath, all covered with water.

He had spent most of Tuesday night at the roadblock in South Shawnee, trying to keep fools and looters out of the evacuated area, thankful it wasn't an everyday part of a detective's job. He'd barely managed a couple hours' sleep before they called him out again. The flood level had dropped by morning, but it had left behind a slick layer of mud atop everything. It was all he could do to keep the car from sliding off the road.

Harter had seen his share of floods, but they'd all been back-porch larcenies compared to this bank heist. He'd never known the river to rage as high and vengeful as it had the night before. Only people who lived among skyscrapers could philosophize about the benevolence of nature, he decided. It was obvious to him that Mother Nature could turn into a mean bitch whenever she damn well chose.

Until yesterday, the worst hit he'd personally witnessed had been when a hurricane—*was it Hazel or some other witch?*—crash-landed in the city. He'd been about twelve, and even though his home on Grant Avenue hadn't been near the river or any of the places you'd expect might flood, the water had run down the hill to the yard and lain for days in low spots. The old people had watched it and announced, *Don't worry. This is nothing like '36.*

But last night . . . This one had all the signs of the 1936 Flood, *the Big One*, six years before he'd been born, the one the old people endlessly told tales of.

Harter gripped the wheel tighter as he steered through Shantytown's narrow streets, past small frame dwellings that seemed to have been there forever, past yards littered with a deposit of soggy debris. Some people called the section "Riverview" now, a classier name that he'd never gotten used to. It had been Shantytown when he was a kid, and it was still Shantytown to him.

From the filthy bathtub ring on some of the walls, he could tell the flood hadn't reached very deep into the residences on the upper side of the street. But the ones on the lower side, nearer the canal, looked like they'd never be lived in again. Most of them had survived 1936, and 1924, too, when the canal had been knocked out.

From old photos, he knew the lower side of Egypt Street had been lined with homes and Shawnee & Chesapeake Canal structures until the '24 Flood had scooted some of them downriver. Then in '36 more had swum away, or been demolished later. He couldn't prove it, but he felt it was the lack of buildings near the river, not the flood control walls, that kept the destruction down in the old canal neighborhood.

In Shantytown, the river bent tight around the Shawnee & Chesapeake Canal, or vice versa, depending on which side you were on. There were places along the towpath where the canal didn't exactly mimic the river's course, but here the two just about kissed. Wednesday morning, the river still rushed over the canal path, discouraging hikers and bikers. Impromptu streams cut channels in the mudpie field between Egypt Street and the towpath. Trees along the riverbank had been leveled by the flood's force as if drunken loggers had blitzkrieged through by night.

Up ahead, he saw the parked squad cars. His tires churned the soft muck as he pulled in behind them. He noticed the heating-oil smell as soon as he opened the door. People had just filled up with fuel for the winter, and then their basement tanks had been deluged.

He hadn't taken three steps across the street before he cussed himself for not bringing hipboots. Squishing on, he headed toward the old house. If there were steps down to it, he couldn't find them. He battled to keep his balance as he slid down the bank. Near the porch he stopped and studied the high-water line on the wall. The entire first floor must have been an indoor swimming pool only a few hours earlier.

He turned left and slogged around the two-story structure until he could see the men waiting for him behind it. Beyond them, across the field, he noticed, most of the power lines were down. Where the lines still stretched taut, raggy clothing hung from the wires. Even though he had seen it himself last night, he found it hard to believe the river had gotten so high.

"What is it, Pete?" the detective asked when he was within earshot.

There were three of them—two cops in splattered uniforms and Pete Epstein, the city medical examiner. Shovels in their hands, they stood near a heap of brown, slimy earth.

The medical examiner shook his head. "You really want to know, Harter?"

"You giving me a choice?"

"We could bury them again," said Epstein, wearily nodding toward his feet.

Toward a collection of bones.

The morning sun was as shit-tinged as everything else in sight.

... 2 ...

"What's it look like?"

"A dead person," said Pete Epstein, flashing a trace of smile.

"Thanks a lot, Doc."

"Hell, Harter, look at them. Those damn bones need a good washing before I can even handle them. Besides, we're still digging them up. I can't tell you much of anything yet."

Harter was amazed he felt nothing as he stared down at the muddy bones. It wasn't like seeing a human being mangled in a car accident. There was nothing really human about the bones at all. No flesh. No blood. No clue as to what kind of person they'd been, whether old or young, good looking or ugly, rich or poor. Nothing to be affected by. Only bones next to a hole that was slowly filling with seepage.

"How long have they been in the ground?"

The short, gray-haired medical examiner shrugged. "Long enough for the body to rot. I told you, I'm not sure of anything. This is going to take a considerable amount of work. I may have to find a specialist. You know, when archaeologists date bones, they're thrilled to be in the right century. Of course, if you want to take over this excavation, I can go back to my office and get started."

7

Harter sidestepped the offer. "Who reported them?"

Epstein pointed across the street to a house painted a sickly green. "Their name's Spilky. The Red Cross suggested they evacuate last night, so they slept at a friend's. When they came back this morning, they were relieved to find their place only had water in the basement. They say they decided to walk around the neighborhood and check out the damage. Apparently there used to be a shed or an outbuilding here, and they noticed it had washed away. When they came down for a look, Mrs. Spilky spotted the top of the skull shining through the mud. As you can see, the flood took off most of the topsoil between here and the river. The phones are all messed up from the flood, so they went back to their friend's and called headquarters. They were waiting for us when we arrived. Just went over to their house a few minutes ago."

"And you found the skull showing, like they said?"

"Yeah. What are you thinking? You suggesting they planted the skeleton? Go over and talk to them. You don't trust anyone, do you?"

"I try not to."

"I don't see any reason to doubt their story. The Spilkys say they've lived on Egypt Street for only ten or eleven months. However old these bones are, they're older than that. And I don't figure anyone kept them in the attic and dropped them here when the flood came along."

"So, someone buried a body here years ago in a shed that washed away yesterday."

"That's my best guess. Anyone burying a body around here would do well to do it inside the shed so no one dug it up by accident, gardening or something. Besides, bury it outside in the open and all the neighbors could watch."

Harter scanned the area. The house stood naked from three sides, with vacant lots to its left and right. Behind was the swamp of a field, stretching flat to the canal and the river. Epstein was right, as he often was. If a person sat on one of the porches across the street, he'd have a top-dollar view of everything that went on.

For the hell of it, Harter said, "Of course, there's no assurance the bones weren't here before the shed."

"No," said Epstein, playing along. "And they built the pyramids by chance over long-dead pharaohs, too. God, Harter, if I really wanted to dig for osteal relics, I'd pick a more exotic location. Damn, *Egypt Street.* No pyramids, lost temples, or belly dancers around here. No walls with hieroglyphics. You should at least get a jaunt to Africa out of a job like this. I just hope it doesn't rain ten more inches before we're through."

"A lot of people are hoping it won't rain for ten months, Pete. Any idea who owns this house?"

"Mr. Spilky says it's been empty the whole time they've lived over there. The kids tell tales about the place being haunted."

Harter glanced down at the bones again. "Maybe it is. When can I expect a report?"

"One of these days."

"I'll be holding my breath," said Harter as he turned and started to make his way back up to the street.

● ● ●

The old man had moved a kitchen chair out on the porch and was sitting on it, watching the cops dig over at the Wilton place. Being outside wasn't too bad. It was just as chilly inside his damp house as it was outdoors. The electricity was dead, and down in the basement, the furnace had flooded. At least the temperature had inched near fifty, so he could live with it without his blood freezing solid.

9

Curry was sure the guy walking up the bank to Egypt Street was a cop like the others, even if he wasn't wearing a uniform and his car didn't have a "Shawnee Police Department" symbol. The fellow had on jeans and a black jacket, but the old man recognized the gait of a policeman in the way the erect six-footer carried himself. The guy seemed to be heading toward the McCoy house—*no, it was the Spilky house now.* Curry never could keep it straight. He still wasn't used to his new neighbors.

The cop was hiking across the muddy street when he looked up and made eye contact with the old man. He immediately changed course and headed toward the porch. "Terrible day, isn't it?" he asked as he neared the messy steps.

"I'm too damn old for high water," said Curry.

"Everyone's too old for high water. Looks like you made it through all right."

"No heat, no lights, no phone, and a cellar to pump out, but, yeah, I made it. Always have."

"Did you spend the night here?"

"No. The Red Cross came and got me and took me up to East Shawnee High School. I slept on a damn cot in the gymnasium and came home this morning. Wasn't the best night I ever spent."

"I suppose not. I guess you've noticed all the activity across the street?"

"Been watching it," mumbled Curry. He knew the small talk was now out of the way and the cop was settling down to business.

"My name is Edward Harter. I'm a detective with the city police."

"Matt Curry. It's Matthew Mark Curry, if you want to be formal. My mother named me for the gospels. If I'd had a brother, she'd have called him Luke John."

"What's happened is we've found a body over there," said

the detective, this Harter. "Actually, I can't say it's much of a body. We found some bones. They've apparently been in the ground a long time. Any idea who owns that house? I could look it up on tax records, but I figured you might know."

"Guess it's still owned by the Wiltons."

"The Wiltons?"

"They've owned it as far back as I remember. An old canal family, like mine. See, that started out as a company-built house, like most everything else on the other side of the street, not that there's much still standing on the lower side of the street anymore."

"There's less now, isn't there? Didn't there used to be a shed back where they're digging?"

"Until last night there was. I helped Wheat Wilton build the thing myself. Must have been the spring of 1941 or so, a year or two before he got married. You could have guessed we put up the shed after '36. It never would have withstood that flood, either."

"Wheat Wilton was the one who lived over there?" asked the cop.

"His real name was Bartley, but he hated it, so he always went by his middle moniker, Wheat. It was his mother's maiden name."

"Is he still alive?"

Curry nodded.

"Does he live around here?"

"Last I knew, he was staying with his daughter on the Avenue. He moved in with her about five years ago, after he retired from the railroad."

"So, what is he, seventy or seventy-one?"

"Yeah. Same as me, give or take a year."

"Are there other Wiltons around—people who would have lived over there? Children, maybe?"

"There was the daughter, and a boy, Roger. He left town in the sixties and I haven't seen him in years."

"What's the daughter's name?"

"Dorothy. Dorothy Merrill, it would be. Husband's Bill, if I recall. His daddy used to work on the railroad with me. I think Bill caught on at the steel mill. Don't know what he does now that the damn mill locked its doors."

Curry watched Harter take a notepad and pen from his jacket pocket and scribble *Wheat Wilton, Dorothy Wilton Merrill, Bill Merrill, Roger Wilton*. When he was done writing, the cop asked, "So you worked for the railroad, too, Mr. Curry?"

"Most everyone around here worked for the Shawnee-Potomac, or had some connection with the railroad, didn't they?"

"I guess they did."

"Me, I used to be a conductor," Curry volunteered. It was neutral enough ground. "At least I was until my last few years, when they stuck me in an office over at the yards. Wheat Wilton and me retired about the same time."

"And his house has been empty ever since?"

"Well, for a while they tried to rent it, but they kept getting unreliable people, so they gave up. Then they tried to sell it, but that old house in the floodplain wasn't what anyone would call prime real estate. One day they took the 'For Sale' sign down and boarded up the windows like you see it."

"I understand the kids in the neighborhood claim it's haunted."

"I don't know what the kids say anymore. Hell, it ain't haunted to me, if that's what you're interested in. I remember when the place was filled with real, live, flesh-and-blood folks."

"Whatever happened to Mrs. Wilton?"

"She died in Nineteen sixty-seven. It's not her in the ground over there, if you're leading that way. She was hit by a truck. Right in the middle of Egypt Street there. I don't believe they ever caught who did it."

The detective's pen was scratching again. When he looked up, he asked, "How about the people next door? The name's Spilky, isn't it? They're the ones who found the bones. Apparently they came home this morning and noticed the shed had washed away, so they went over for a look-see. I take it they've lived in Shantytown less than a year."

"Can't quarrel with any of that. Me, when I came back this morning, the police cars were already parked out front and the men were already digging. You'll have to go talk to the Spilkys yourself."

"I plan to." Harter flipped his notebook closed and returned it to his pocket. "Look, I don't mean to sound stupid, but you've lived here a long time. You don't have any idea who might be buried over there, do you?"

Curry shrugged. "Depends."

"On what?"

"On how long those bones have been a-moldering in the ground. You could have someone who died in a canal feud a hundred years ago, or a person drowned in the Nineteen twenty-four Flood when there were loads of canal people out in the water, trying to keep the boats from propelling downstream. Whether anyone was stuck in the mud in that very spot, I can't tell you. I was just a kid."

"Remember," said Harter, "the body was buried *beneath* the shed."

Curry went on just the same. "Christ, you could even have what's left of some hippie hiker. Ever since they made the towpath a park, there's been all sorts of strangers hiking and biking it. Any one of them could have buried a body beside a vacant house. God knows some of the things that might have hap-

13

pened in Shantytown down the years. Of course, this isn't the same place it used to be, if you ask me. It's not the place people recall it was. Hell, Shawnee as a whole isn't what it used to be, either. They're turning the passenger station into a museum, like they turned the canal into a park. That's what they do when things die, isn't it? Why, they could turn this whole section into a Shawnee Flood Museum some day."

The cop smiled. "Maybe they'll hire you as a tour guide."

"Why not? Give me a chance to earn a little money. See that mud line on the step, just below the porch?"

Harter nodded.

"You probably can't make it out good, but beneath all the garbage is a mark my mother scratched in 'thirty-six. And just below that's another she scratched in 'twenty-four. Last night the water got to exactly the same spot it did fifty years ago. No, it'd be forty-nine years ago, wouldn't it? Saint Patrick's Day, Nineteen thirty-six. If this goddamned flood could have held off four more months, we could have had a real fiftieth-anniversary celebration. In Nineteen thirty-six my mother stood on this porch and tried to sweep the water away. She got pneumonia out of it and died."

The detective was silent for a moment. He probably didn't know what to say. Then, he reached in his pocket, produced a card, and handed it up to Curry. "If something happens to come back to you, Mr. Curry—something that could have to do with the bones—get in touch with me."

"I will," promised the old man.

He was still reading Harter's title and phone number when the cop walked across the yard to the McCoy place—no, the Spilky place.

... 3 ...

Matt Curry felt like he'd made some progress by the end of the day. The electric company men had been on the scene fast and had repaired the downed lines by dark. While they'd worked along the river, a fire truck had showed up and firemen had pumped out his basement. The utility inspector, who had come to check the wiring in his house, reported it was okay to use the lights, but warned against using the furnace until it got a good once-over. Word was, the phone company would have things going in a day or two.

About 9:30 a Red Cross man knocked on his door to offer a ride back to the high school gym for the night. Curry turned him down, and before long the guy was back with a small electric heater that he said could at least heat the bedroom. He promised a volunteer crew would arrive in the next few days to help with the house and basement.

Upstairs, as he plugged in the heater, Curry wondered if he was getting all this attention simply because he was old. Space heaters, volunteer work crews, cots in high school gyms . . . It hadn't been like that in 1936. Then, they'd had to fend for themselves.

He told himself he could still fend for himself. The house

might be cold and damp, a disaster zone to the Red Cross, but it was his home. He didn't intend to spend another night tossing and turning in a gymnasium, a few feet away from someone he scarcely knew or didn't know at all. Besides, if everyone left, Egypt Street would be a sitting duck for thieves and vandals. They hadn't had as much of a crime problem in 1936. People were different then. He hoped the cops still planned to patrol the area. Whether or not they did, no one would break into his house without a fight.

Most of the other dwellings on the street had been dark for hours, their owners choosing to sleep in more comfort. The Spilkys, next door, had puttered around for a while after the detective left, but before the weak sun had given up altogether, they'd departed for the night.

Curry climbed into bed fully dressed and pulled the old quilts up over him. He knew he'd be tossing and turning again, even in his own bed.

He'd been outside trying to clean off the porch steps when the diggers had left the Wilton place. They'd carried a green plastic garbage bag to the police car, and Curry had known full well what was in it. *The bones.* The past was surfacing. The detective had known it would. That's why Harter had left his card and asked him to be in touch if he recalled anything. Cops had their tricks.

Harter had said the kids believed the Wilton place was haunted. He guessed, in some way, they were right. *It was haunted.* But not by a ghost. Not by some mysterious lantern-swinging headless specter along the canal.

Like his own, the Wilton house was one of those 1890s Shantytown frame structures, two stories high, built by boatmen and mule drivers so they could stare out on the towpath, their livelihood, just as railroaders once built homes facing the tracks.

Shantytown. The name had been coined by people who'd

lived in more prosperous sections to designate the conglomeration of buildings where the canal families lived and labored. The place had never been as shabby as its name. Wheat Wilton's house wasn't anything Curry would call a shanty, and neither was his. Shanties didn't last a century and survive floods.

Those houses had actually outlasted the Shawnee & Chesapeake Canal Company itself. Sometimes Curry wondered whether he'd have ended up working on the canal if it hadn't been knocked out of business by the 1924 Flood. Or so went the story. Hell, the flood hadn't been the culprit. The railroad was. The canal just couldn't compete and had been in decline for years even by 1924. As far back as Curry could picture, hulls of rotting flatboats had lain along the towpath. He and Wheat had played among the Shawnee & Chesapeake ruins, pretending to be flatboat captains.

Curry's father had been a real captain. Then, one day, his old man hadn't returned from a trip downriver. The boat had come home, but no one had any notion what had become of his father. They'd never heard from him again. Maybe he ran off to California. To Curry, anyone who up and left beat it to California. He'd been six years old at the time. His mother, who'd always had a Bible-quoting streak, suddenly came down with religion and suffered waves of its attacks for the rest of her life.

Curry would have loved to have been a boat captain. Would have loved to work on a Mississippi steamboat like his hero, Mark Twain. Envied his father the chance to jump ship downriver and go off to see the world. Go off to California. But the canal shut down, so when it came time to get a job, he signed on with the Shawnee-Potomac Railroad, the canal's nemesis. He hadn't seen the world, but he had seen a lot of whistle-stops.

Wheat, too, had gotten a railroad job, but now the railroad seemed to be going the way of the canal. If he was a young man, Curry guessed it would be tough to get a good Shawnee-Potomac job. The station was going to be a museum. The detective hadn't sounded like he liked the changes much, either.

Curry turned onto his side and closed his eyes to make another stab at sleep.

He'd never become a captain, no matter what he'd dreamed when he was young.

WHEN HE WAS YOUNG.

When he was a boy, there was a house he'd believed was just as haunted in its own way as the Wilton place apparently was to kids today. This one had been just outside the city limits, and three old people had lived in it. Two aged men, probably brothers from the look of them—both tall and creaky—and an equally old woman, short and plump as a Thanksgiving turkey. He could never decide which of the brothers the woman was married to, if, indeed, she was married to either.

The house was a bare wood thing with that century-old, seen-it-all air, and the three old people were just as weathered.

The woman always had on one of those homemade dresses with little pink and white checks and an apron tied over it. The men wore overalls, no matter what the season. Sometimes in summer they'd be bare bony-chested, like maybe they weren't wearing anything beneath the denim. Out in the mountains, he'd seen old boys who went around like that, no underwear or anything. He guessed those guys were really a pair of old country boys, and the place was really a farm, or had been once upon a time, but even sixty years before, Shawnee was encroaching on them, city houses nibbling away at their hilly pasture.

On Sunday afternoons, his Uncle John would take Curry and his own kids for a ride out to the woods, and whenever they passed the place, one of the old trio was outside. Wood smoke always poured from their chimney, for heat in icebound January, for cooking in dog days July.

What struck him—what he still remembered—was that the three never seemed to move. He never saw one of them flex a muscle. It was like they were frozen in place on their porch, or rooted in the ground halfway to the woodpile, or standing on the path to the outhouse, like wax figures in a boardwalk museum.

Even as a kid, he'd known those old people had to move. They were alive, weren't they? They weren't wax figures. After all, when Uncle John's Model T passed them again, the one he'd seen frozen on the path to the outhouse would now be locked in a new position on the way to the chicken coop or somewhere.

He'd been a smart kid and he'd come to understand. Those old people were moving through another time and world, the city be damned. They were moving so slow, like in a dream, so slow that someone young like him, tearing along in a Ford car, was simply traveling too fast to be able to spot their movement.

Hell.

WHEN HE WAS YOUNG.

Now he was old, and his house was an old house, its cellar flooded too many times. The kids thought the people and places he'd known were haunted.

Those kids, if they bothered to notice him at all, probably glanced over and wondered, "Doesn't that son of a bitch ever move?"

He was the one frozen on the path to the outhouse.

Not always so.

WHEN HE WAS YOUNG.

She was wearing a dress so thin you could see her body move through it. She smelled so clean.

··· 4 ···

"I shot her."

Too damn early for this confession stuff, thought Harter, taking a hit of coffee to sharpen himself up. Wednesday night, for the second night straight, he'd volunteered to guard Shantytown streets against the crazies. It seemed like he'd hardly gotten home before Herr, the desk cop, had called him down to headquarters.

"I shot her."

Darrell Phillips had simply strolled in early that morning and announced he'd murdered his wife. The guy's voice was amazingly calm, but his fingers gave away his nervousness. His pale, puffy palm was cupped over his face like a prayer cloth, shielding his eyes. The fat fingers kneaded at his forehead, over and over and over.

"Drink some coffee. It'll help bring you around," said Harter, pointing across the table at a white Styrofoam cup. He didn't know if it was really possible to bring Phillips around, to clear his brain, or not. He had no idea how much Phillips was going to tell him, or even if he'd understood the rights that had been read to him. He just hoped he could keep Phillips talking until McManaway came back with a report on what he'd found.

Phillips kept his face low as he moved his hand away from his forehead to reach for the cup. Still, Harter managed to snatch a flash of his dazed eyes—*his completely dazed eyes.* Odds were, the man didn't even realize he was sitting in the interrogation room of the Shawnee Police Department.

"Okay, let's start again. You run an appliance store by the viaduct, and you live in an apartment over top of it, right?"

Phillips' head bobbed like he understood. His fingertips rubbed at the Styrofoam cup like they were still rubbing at his own skin.

Harter figured the appliance dealer was in his late thirties, but it was hard to judge. Phillips' heavy belly and balding dome made him seem older. He'd probably looked middle aged since his twenties.

"Why did you shoot your wife?"

Phillips' fingernails grated lightly against the Styrofoam.

Harter tried again. "The two of you have a fight? Were you drunk?"

Nothing but that damn dazed—*dazing*—stare. You couldn't even call it glassy. Plastic was more like it.

Sweat was rolling down the guy's face, though the room was far from hot. Phillips didn't even lift his head when the knock on the door came and Dave McManaway finally peeked in.

"You been to the apartment?" Harter asked the beat cop.

McManaway nodded and motioned the detective out into the hall. As he rose from the table, Harter told Phillips, "Work on your coffee. I'll be right back. Try to relax."

He'd barely stepped into the corridor and shut the door behind him before McManaway was saying in a weird tone, "Detective Edward Harter, meet Mrs. Darrell Phillips."

"Vi Phillips," she said, without extending her hand. "Is my husband in there?"

"Your husband?" Harter didn't believe it.

"Darrell."

"Darrell? Yeah, he's in there." He glanced over at McManaway. It was surely too early in the morning for this goddamn charade.

"I didn't know what to do," explained McManaway, "so I brought her to headquarters with me. I sent Clark and the others home."

"I'd like to see Darrell," said Vi Phillips.

"Wait a minute. Let me get this straight. You do understand your husband has confessed to murdering you last night?"

"The officer told me. Obviously, Darrell didn't murder me, Detective."

"He says he shot you. He didn't wave a gun around or anything, did he?"

"Darrell doesn't even own a gun. I hate them. I won't allow him to keep one in either the store or the apartment. He doesn't have one with him, does he?"

"No," mumbled Harter, turning back to Dave McManaway.

"We didn't find a gun or any evidence of shooting. We didn't find anything unusual at all. When we got there, the store and apartment were locked up tight and the lights were off. Mrs. Phillips was still in bed. We woke her up, and while she dressed, Clark and I scouted the place. Everything appeared to be in order."

"Everything *was* in order," piped up Vi Phillips, her irritation showing.

Her eyes were a little red, like she'd been jolted out of a peaceful sleep and into a nightmare. She'd clearly dressed fast. Underneath her coat, the top button of her floral print dress was unfastened. Her dyed red hair was uncombed. She was in her thirties, decided Harter, confirming his estimate of her husband's age.

"Was your husband at home all last night?" he asked.

"Except when he was at the warehouse."

"The warehouse?"

"We lease a building by the river in Shantytown, or River-view, or whatever they call it. We keep extra appliances in it, and do some of our repair work there. The building flooded Tuesday night, along with everything else. Darrell spent most of yesterday checking on the damage and trying to salvage what he could. He came home about nine."

"Was he upset?"

"Of course he was upset, Detective. He said we'd lost thousands of dollars' worth of stuff. And it wasn't insured. Flood insurance is expensive, and when was the last time the area flooded like that? Darrell was real depressed when he came back to the apartment."

"When he got home, did he start drinking, or was he testy, trying to pick a fight?"

"Darrell hardly ever drinks," she said, arching her back again at the suggestion that anything serious might be wrong. "I don't see what business all of this is of yours."

"Look, lady, I didn't call up your husband and invite him down here at this hour and suggest he cook up a story about shooting you. He did it on his own. I'm trying to find out why. Is he violent? Has he acted strange before?"

"How do you define *strange*, Detective?"

"However you'd define it, Mrs. Phillips. You know him better than anyone else."

"He can be moody, if that's what you mean."

"Moody?"

"Depressed, that's all. It's like something will trip him, a bit of news or something. The flood was just too much. But, no, he isn't violent. He's simply been under a big weight lately, trying to keep the business going. All these big discount stores make it hard on little stores like ours. I've told him, if worst comes to worst, we can close up and find other jobs, but you know how it is. Once you've worked for yourself, it's difficult to consider working for someone else. His father started the business, and Darrell feels like a failure because he hasn't been successful with it."

"What's he do when he gets depressed?"

"He might just stare at the TV, or sometimes he talks about Vietnam."

"What about Vietnam?"

"About how much he hated being there in the war. Look, Detective Harter, can I see him? I'd really like to take him home and put him to bed."

"I'm not sure that's smart, Mrs. Phillips," said Harter, stalling for time to decide what to do. "I've got to consider your safety, and the safety of others."

"No one has anything to fear from Darrell. You can see he didn't kill me. He's never raised a hand at me. I've told you he doesn't own a gun. You haven't charged him with anything, have you?"

"Not yet."

"So you've no reason to keep him locked up."

"He's not exactly locked up. He's sitting in there, drinking coffee."

"Do I have to call our lawyer?"

"I think he needs a doctor more than he needs a lawyer. He could have a mental problem."

"Not Darrell," she insisted.

Harter pictured Phillips sitting tensely at the interrogation table, rubbing his forehead, rubbing the Styrofoam, talking about murdering his wife. He played out the bluff. "We could send him over to Shawnee Mental Health Center for a day or two of evaluation. I'd feel better not just letting him walk out on

24

the street without some assurance that he's not going to do something."

Vi Phillips' eyes were wide open now, and Harter felt McManaway staring at him, too.

"He won't do anything terrible. I'll see to that," she said.

"I don't want to be the one to vouch for him."

"Darrell—" She broke off whatever she was about to say and seemed to reconsider. "It's only stress, you see. He's . . . He *has* been seeing a doctor off and on . . . a psychiatrist . . . I'll set up another appointment."

"Soon."

"Soon," she agreed. "Now, will you let me see him? Can I take him home?"

Before he showed his hand, Harter made her wait two long, silent minutes to let the seriousness sink in. Then he slowly opened the door to the interrogation room. "Mr. Phillips, your wife has come for you."

He watched the guy's face carefully for a flinch, for a reaction of some sort. What happened surprised him. Darrell Phillips raised his head and was open-faced and smiling. "Hi, Vi," he said as he stood up.

"The car's outside," she told him.

As the couple walked down the hall, McManaway asked Harter, in a voice that was almost a whisper, "You think you did the right thing?"

"How the hell do I know?"

"You sure she'll take him for treatment?"

"I'm not sure of anything."

"Pretty crummy way to start the day."

"Yeah. Tuesday, the flood. Wednesday, the bones. Now this." Harter lit a cigarette. "I guess the day has to start some way."

... 5 ...

From across the desk, Harter read the upside-down headline in the newspaper that Dave McManaway was devouring. Christ, Pete Epstein always had been a publicity hound. He should have seen it coming.

McManaway caught his stare. "What do you think of all this?"

"I think it must sell papers. Now that the river's gone down, it gives reporters something to write about. As many people will read that story as read about the flood in the first place."

He reached over, took the paper, and studied the front-page photo. The soggy old Wilton house looked gray and gloomy enough to be haunted. His eyes ran down the column, seeking facts, but found none, only the tabloid-style headline. Epstein had told the press that the bones were those of a woman, but the other details had to wait until an expert from the state university traveled to Shawnee on Saturday.

"It'll take all the expertise I can gather to pinpoint this thing. We need good leads before we can check dental records

26

and that sort of thing. It's quite a mystery," Epstein the show-man was quoted as expounding. "There's such a margin of error when dating old bones that we're still only guessing. It's all ball-park stuff, but I'd be looking at from about Nineteen forty-five to, say, Nineteen seventy. The police should be sifting through reports of missing women from that time period."

Topnotch advice giver, Pete Epstein. *The police should be sifting through reports.* Harter shook off the advice, inhaled more cof-fee, and glanced over at the gray metal filing cabinets lining a wall of the office. Hell of a lot of reports to sift.

McManaway must have been watching him closely, for he asked, "How do you go back and decide what happened so long ago?"

"Got me."

"I bet you wish Caruthers hadn't taken the month off."

"I don't give a damn. I'm glad he's taking his sick leave and vacation time. I won't cry when he retires December thirty-first."

"You really don't like him, do you?"

No, Harter didn't like Caruthers and never had, but he hadn't realized his distaste for the other detective was so appar-ent. He wondered how many of the other beat cops were aware of it, and whether it was a hot topic of conversation.

Year after year, as they'd shared an office, playing detec-tive, his dislike for Caruthers had deepened. He knew it was irrational, and he'd tried to dampen his smile when Caruthers had announced his retirement and lit out for Florida to eat up his accumulated leave.

"He left you at a rough time, didn't he? Left you by your-self, and now we've got a flood and an old mystery," said McManaway, obviously trying to open Harter up.

Harter lit another cigarette and stared back at the filing cabinets that Caruthers had so diligently filled with paper. He'd been more than good at red tape, more than making up for Harter's hatred of it. Caruthers would already be sifting through the old reports for accounts of missing women, as Epstein had suggested.

"You did put in for Caruthers' job, didn't you?" he asked McManaway.

"Yeah."

"Good."

Ever since the young cop had first helped Harter on a stake-out, Dave McManaway had been his first choice for detective. That was why Harter had delegated him to lead the team who'd gone to the Phillips apartment that morning. He wanted to ease McManaway into detective work, wanted chances to praise him to the chief.

"Did you read about the teenagers?" asked McManaway, changing the subject. He must have realized he'd hit a dead end with questions about Caruthers.

"No."

"Seems a seventeen-year-old boy and a sixteen-year-old girl were parked by the river on Tuesday night when the water came up. They felt their car lift off the ground and start to float away. Somehow they managed to roll down the windows and jump out. When they got to high ground, they ran to the nearest house for help. Must have been a sight when the people opened the door. All the boy had on was his socks, and she wasn't wearing anything. They claimed they stripped so they could swim better."

Harter laughed. "God, imagine telling your father how you lost the car. Expensive date. I remember how hard it was just to explain how the radio antenna caught on a tree limb and snapped off one night when I parked in the woods. Those kids must have been cold. It was down in the thirties Tuesday night."

McManaway tossed his Styrofoam cup in the trash and

stood up. "Hell, you know it could have happened to me when I was seventeen. Could have been me parked along the river with Sally. Funny, what stays in your mind."

Harter watched the younger cop go out the door. *Funny, what stays in your mind.* McManaway was right. His mind was certainly crowded with junk. He was sifting through the debris when the first call came.

The guy's voice had the creak of age in it, and for a second he thought it might be Matt Curry—Matthew Mark Curry of biblical name. But it wasn't Curry with some retrieved fact. It was another old fellow who, without prodding, poured out a saga of the Shawnee & Chesapeake Canal so rapidly that Harter was immediately confused. He managed to rein the guy to a halt and back him up for a cleaner start.

"They're my brother's bones. He fell off a canal boat in Nineteen fourteen, when he was twelve. We always were told it took place near Shawnee. They probably buried him along the towpath. Jimmy was taken on by a boat captain to drive the mules, and it was only his second trip when he fell off, hit his head, and drowned. My mother keened for weeks. She never did get over it completely."

"I'll take your name and number, but I have to tell you, we believe it's a woman's skeleton," said Harter when he could pry in a word. "We don't think the bones are that old, either."

No matter, the guy launched into the tale anew with a few fresh details. "A young fellow like you's got no notion how it was along the canal," the old boy informed him.

When he was tired of listening, Harter pulled his perennial con game of saying he had an emergency call on another line, and hung up. He had the feeling the trick would come in handy over the days ahead.

He learned from callers that the story had been carried coast to coast on the wire service that morning. Hundreds of papers had printed it under headlines like MURDER VICTIM UN-COVERED BY APPALACHIAN FLOOD. Who cared if there was no proof whether the woman had actually been murdered? He found it irritating that at least three dozen people had drowned, been washed away, or were still missing in what they'd taken to calling the Killer Flood of '85, yet less than two days later the headlines were grabbed by an unknown skeleton that had been buried for twenty, thirty, maybe even forty years.

The phone rang again. A nearly hysterical woman from Chicago said her daughter had hiked the Shawnee & Chesapeake Canal in 1975 and had never returned. The family had lived in Baltimore then, and her daughter would have been thirty. She'd had a string of bad luck—an abusive husband, a divorce, arguments with relatives, finally an accident that had left her crippled. She'd been determined to hike the entire towpath as a test of survival.

Harter groaned. Old Matt Curry had said the bones could belong to a hiker, and now, here one was. A transient hiker. The worst possible case. God knows what kind of crazy bastard she could have met along the line.

He immediately called Pete Epstein and repeated the woman's story.

"She's not the one," Epstein assured him. "This was a relatively young woman and I haven't seen any sign of an injured leg. I don't find any evidence of broken bones at all. Besides, Nineteen seventy-five is probably too late, unless I'm way off base. Like I told the papers, I should know more after Saturday."

"Great of you to tell the press more than you told me," said Harter.

"Hell, they called me. Don't bitch. I run an open office. This isn't national security. If a reporter asks me a question, I answer it. I like to stay on the good side of those people. Didn't anyone ever tell you not to argue with folks who buy ink by the gallon?"

"You still interested in politics, Pete? Building up points? What are you running for? President or just governor?"

"I want to be king," said Epstein.

When they were through firing volleys, Harter dialed the woman in Chicago and informed her the bones weren't likely to be her daughter's. That chore out of the way, he sorted again through the names and numbers piling up on his desk. Amazing, how people in the Midwest or New England had ties to Shawnee, with its population of less than forty thousand, and counting down each day as the jobs dwindled. Amazing, how many people felt the unexplained tragedies of their lives might have something to do with those bones.

He knew the chief would love the long distance bill this case was going to rack up. He could already hear the clamor. The chief was so budget conscious these days that he'd refused to even consider hiring a replacement for Caruthers until Caruthers had worked off all his leave time. So Harter was left to answer the phone alone.

And the phone rang.

Caller after caller convinced him that, no matter how plain the facts in the news might be, people would read whatever they wanted to read into them. If they knew of a missing boy, they ignored the fact that the bones were those of a woman. If they knew of a disappearance in 1925, they ignored Pete Epstein's estimate of the date. If they knew of a girl who never came home from a hike on the towpath, they forgot the damn canal was more than 180 miles long and Shawnee was just a port on its western end.

A college student verified the theory. He was positive the skeleton was of an Indian, a Shawnee or a Delaware who'd died three hundred or more years before. Turned out the flood had uncovered what was believed to be an Indian village on the South Branch of the Potomac in West Virginia, and the student figured it might have done the same in Shantytown. He wanted the inside track on studying the remains.

"I doubt it was Pocahontas in the shed," said Harter, almost slamming down the phone. A minute later he felt bad about his anger. He usually wasn't as clipped and angry. The flood, the skeleton, the sad and crazy appliance dealer, the calls, the hours of night patrol . . . they were getting to him.

Liz was getting to him, too. Or the growing distance between them was. He tried not to talk or think about her, but every time his mind wasn't on work, it was on her, and what was going wrong. Not that he could put what was going wrong into words. He'd stopped talking about her to friends because they all expected him to voice some reason why things were stormy. But the words were only about symptoms, not causes, and so he rarely said them. Kept them in. Early on, someone had told him, "Time is a healer." People always seemed to have an old saying or easy platitude to pass on, just like they always wanted a reason. *Time is a healer*, and maybe it was at times, but sometimes it was just time. Just as well they kept calling him out to work. Just as well he didn't have long hours to sit in his apartment and think about her.

He got up, walked over to a filing cabinet, pulled open a drawer, stared at a row of files. Caruthers would have relished the chance to stay off the street a while. There was no danger in the office. Caruthers had actually enjoyed sitting at his gray metal government desk and filling out reports. But Caruthers was gone and soon would be gone for good. Harter tried to convince himself that sifting through files was a small price to pay. It was a small price to pay for not thinking about Liz, too.

When the phone rang again, he gave serious consideration

to playing deaf. But, the ever-dutiful cop, he hoisted the receiver, introduced himself, and, pen poised over notepad, waited.

"Her name was Brenda Keith, and she disappeared at the end of the war, about Nineteen forty-five."

Harter perked up. Right sex, right year. "Why are you so sure it's her?" he asked.

"I guess I don't know for sure. I can't prove anything, but it could be her."

God, the guy's even reasonable.

"Well, tell me, what makes you think it might be this Brenda Keith?"

"I was married to her back then. When I went into the army in Nineteen forty-two, I left her in Shawnee. I never got another letter from her after Christmas of 'forty-four. She was nowhere to be found when I got home. Our landlord said she just disappeared one day. No one could tell me anything about what became of her."

"Then your name's Keith?"

The man paused a moment before answering. "Paul Keith."

"You still live here in Shawnee?"

"No, Pittsburgh. I read about the skeleton in the paper this morning. It's been eating at me all day. I know where the Wilton house is. We only lived about two blocks from it."

"So you knew the Wiltons in those days?"

"I was aware of who they were. We never visited them or anything. Brenda was raised in Shantytown, so she knew most everyone. I moved to Shawnee for work during the Depression."

No one moves to Shawnee for work anymore, thought Harter. But what he asked was: "Did she know the Wiltons very well? Did she ever talk about them?"

"I've been trying to remember, and just can't. It was forty years ago, a long time, another life ago."

"How old would your wife have been in Nineteen forty-five?"

"She was nineteen and I was twenty when we got married in 'forty-one. That would make her twenty-two or twenty-three when I lost track of her."

"Can you give me a description?"

"She was about five foot four, and blond, real blond. Look, I'm not even sure why I called. The newspaper story just drug it all back up. I left Shawnee in Nineteen forty-seven and moved here to Pittsburgh to start over again. I . . . I've got a whole new family and a new life now. I don't want them to get involved in this. My wife has no idea I was married before. I just thought I should let someone know. It nags at you, year after year. Suddenly, I'm wondering again if Brenda didn't really leave me, but was killed, you know."

"Understand, we don't know how this woman died. But your wife, did she have any relatives or close friends who might still live here? You didn't have any children, did you?"

"No, no children by her. As far as relatives, she was an only child and was raised by an aunt. Brenda never mentioned her parents. I don't think she remembered them."

"What was her aunt's name?"

"Myrt. Myrtle Harris. Harris was Brenda's maiden name, you see. Her aunt Myrt had always lived in Shantytown. She died about Nineteen forty-three, when I was in the service."

"Where did you and your wife live in those days?"

"Fletcher Street . . . One thirteen . . . God, I haven't thought about the place in years. I've tried not to."

"I can understand," said Harter. "I'm sorry it's all coming back to you, but it may be of some help to us. If I turn anything up, I'll contact you."

"Don't—"

"What?"

34

"If my wife answers, don't tell her what it's about. I guess I might have to explain it all to her, but I don't want to if I don't have to."

Harter could hear the ache in Paul Keith's voice even after he'd hung up. *Brenda Keith.* He finally had something worth moving on. And he knew the place to move with it was where he should have gone that afternoon instead of being trapped in the office.

It wasn't yet four o'clock. He still had plenty of time to find Wheat Wilton before he called it a day.

··· 6 ···

Turned out Dorothy and Bill Merrill lived in one of the red brick rowhouses along what everyone in East Shawnee simply referred to as "the Avenue," the long street that linked residential sections with the South Shawnee railroad yards. If you knew what you were searching for, you could still find evidence of the trolley tracks that once ran up the broad old roadway.

The Merrill house had an archway to the left of the front stoop, much like a house Harter had lived in for a while as a kid. Behind its high wooden gate, he knew, was an alleyway that shot the depth of the building, back to the yard and the kitchen door. He wasn't sure whether to knock at the front or go through the arch to the rear. One of the curses of being a cop was constantly walking up to strange houses and being uncertain how to make your entrance, whether to knock at the living room or go around to the kitchen, where he felt he was likely to find Dorothy Merrill cooking supper.

Dorothy Merrill. Dorothy Wilton, it would have been in high school. If she'd grown up in Shantytown, she must have attended East Shawnee High at roughly the same time he had. Yet he could come up with no memory of her. Neither her name nor her husband's meant anything to him. Not that it mattered.

East Shawnee was a large school that drew from half of the city and some of the rural areas outside. He'd never lived in Shantytown. Nor had he been what anyone would call an outgoing student or school leader. There were plenty of people his age he didn't know. If he could have foreseen he'd end up a detective, perhaps he'd have kept detailed notes on his peers. *Fat chance.* On the other hand, Caruthers might have.

He decided to attack the front door, stepped up on the stoop, knocked. The woman who answered was in her early forties and wore blue jeans and a pink T-shirt with SHAWNEE BOMBERS lettered across it.

Dorothy Merrill didn't seem surprised when he informed her who he was and why he'd come. Yes, of course, she'd heard about the skeleton being found where the shed had washed away. The whole thing had given her a chill, but she hadn't called the police because she had nothing to say, no notion whose bones they might be. She hadn't lived on Egypt Street for nearly twenty-five years, not since getting married. Besides, she figured the police would get in touch with her or her husband, and now they had.

Harter detected no strain in her voice or manner. She spoke in a calm, efficient way that inclined him to give her the benefit of any doubt.

The living room was small and cozy, its every surface covered with photos and knickknacks. She must do ceramics, he figured. On top of the television set was a family portrait of a younger Dorothy Merrill, her husband, and two boys, one in his early teens and the other maybe six years old. It was the kind of discount portrait they snapped in front of a screen in the corner of a supermarket. Around the room were framed school photos of the two boys at various ages. On an end table was a picture of an older man.

"Is that your father, Wheat Wilton?" he asked.

"Yeah."

"I was hoping to meet him, hoping to ask him what he might know. He lived on Egypt Street until five years ago, didn't he?"

"That's right. He moved in with us after he retired. The old house was too much for him by himself. I don't think seeing Daddy will do you much good, though."

"Why?"

"He had a stroke two years ago and can barely talk. He's up in his room."

"I'd still like to meet him if I could."

"Well, all right," she said reluctantly. "Come on. Excuse the mess, Detective. Bill and I work odd hours, and we've still got Bart at home. You came at a bad time. I'm running around, trying to get some food together so I can get out of here. Thursday night's my bowling night. They'll all be full of questions about the body being found at Daddy's house. I wish we could have sold that place years ago, but no one bit."

Harter followed the Shawnee Bomber out of the room, down a short hall to a newel post, then up the narrow staircase. Dorothy Merrill was tall and thin, and rather attractive in an untended sort of way, but there was something off center about her face that kept her from being pretty. He wondered if she took after her father or her mother. He had his answer soon enough.

Wheat Wilton was propped on pillows in a chair that was angled toward a second-floor window. He was staring out the glass, out at the Avenue—except, no, he wasn't exactly doing a traffic count—he was just staring, straight out, at the brick wall of the house across the street. He had a full head of shaggy white hair and, like his daughter, was slim and long boned. And there was something lopsided about his face too, or had that been caused by the stroke?

38

The old man showed no sign that he was aware they'd entered the room, not even when Mrs. Merrill said, "Daddy, this man wants to talk to you. He's a police officer."

Harter tried to be as simple and direct as he could. "We've found a skeleton at your house on Egypt Street."

Wheat Wilton didn't budge. The lines on his pale cheeks didn't even gather.

"I came to ask if you know anything about it," continued Harter.

Wheat Wilton didn't budge. He might as well have been a store dummy.

"I told you it wouldn't do any good," said the daughter. "But ask whatever you want. If I can answer for him, I will, though like I said, those bones are news to me. I'm sure they are to Daddy, too."

Maybe not, thought Harter, but there wasn't much use in fishing around, so he went right to the heart. "Did you ever hear of a woman named Brenda Keith? Her maiden name would have been Brenda Harris. She was reported missing from Shantytown at the end of the war."

"End of the war? You mean Vietnam?" asked Dorothy Merrill.

"No, World War Two."

"World War Two? I wouldn't even have been two years old, Detective. What can you remember from when you were two?"

Not a hell of a lot, he agreed, but he plugged on. "Your father would have been around thirty, wouldn't he? He'd have a clear memory."

"You're a little too late to tap his memory. Look at him."

Harter turned to Wheat Wilton again. "Was he in the war?"

"He spent World War Two working for the railroad. That was so long ago—why do you think this Brenda Keith has something to do with it?"

"She's just one possibility. We may come across others. She's supposed to have lived on Fletcher Street with an aunt, Myrtle Harris, before she married a Paul Keith."

Mrs. Merrill shook her head. "Means nothing to me. Surely there are older people in South Shawnee you can ask."

"Like Matt Curry," said Harter.

"Do you know Matt Curry?"

"I met him yesterday when I visited the crime scene."

"Crime scene?" Suddenly she was crossing to the old man in the chair. "Is something the matter, Daddy? Do you want something?"

Wheat Wilton had managed to move his head slightly. Had the mention of Matt Curry forced some wires to connect?

"You're upsetting him, Detective. Haven't we done enough of this? Can't we go back downstairs and leave him in peace?"

"Okay, we can go down. But he seemed to react to Matt Curry's name."

Harter could have sworn the lights lit in Wilton's weak blue eyes.

"Daddy and Matt Curry lived across the street from each other most of their lives," said Dorothy Merrill as she led him from the room to the steps. "They grew up together."

"I take it they were close friends."

"They played together, then both worked for the railroad. It's like, when you're around someone your whole life, what can you say? You know each other too well, maybe. They had their good times, I'm sure, and they had their arguments, particularly as they got older. Old men will feud."

"About what?" asked Harter, following her into the kitchen.

"Whether it's going to rain. I don't know. I told you it's been a long time since I've lived on Egypt Street."

"Has Curry ever come here to visit him?"

40

"No." She turned up the gas under a pot of noodle soup.

"He told me you have a brother named Roger."

"Yeah."

"I'd like to talk to him."

"You're free to talk to him all you want, if you can find him. None of us have seen him since . . . It must have been some time in 1968 when he left Shawnee."

"Any special reason for his leaving?"

"You're full of questions, aren't you, Detective? Only Roger can give you the answers to why he does—why he did—anything. I can't explain him and never could. Neither could Daddy. Roger was four years younger than me. I was born in Nineteen forty-four, and he was born in Nineteen forty-eight. Roger just took off, not long after my mother died. He went to California to be a hippie or something. That's the last we heard of him."

Dorothy Merrill had pale blue eyes like her father, and Harter could sense real anger in them. It was more than simple irritation at his probing as she rushed around getting supper so she could go bowling.

"I understand your mother died in a hit-and-run. Exactly when was it?"

"It was a hit-and-run, all right. December Nineteen sixty-seven, a few weeks before Christmas. They never found the driver. Matt Curry must have told you all sorts of things."

"She must have been, what, forty-five or fifty?"

"She'd just turned forty-four. She was only twenty when I was born, and twenty-five when she had my brother."

"Your father's a good bit older. What's he, about seventy?"

"He'll be seventy-one in February. He was twenty-eight and she was nineteen when they were married, if it means anything."

"You wouldn't happen to have pictures of your mother and brother, would you?"

"Why?"

"Just wondered. I noticed all the family photos in the living room. Since I seem to be rooting around in the past, I'd like to know what the people looked like."

She ladled out a cup of noodle soup. "I don't know where any pictures would be. Probably packed away with Daddy's things." She put the cup on a tray beside a glass of tomato juice, a spoon, and a napkin. Then she flicked off the burner and turned to him again. "If you don't mind, I've got to get Daddy fed so I can get out of here. I can't help you. *We* can't help you. Honest."

"Did you and your brother go to East Shawnee High?"

"Yeah. Why?"

"Just wondered. I don't remember you. Of course, he'd be considerably younger than me, but you're only two years younger."

"Roger graduated in 1966, then went to Shawnee Community College for a while. I quit school in 1961, the start of my senior year, and got married to Bill. I never saw you before, either."

Harter guessed that explained things, but asked, "Did your husband go to East Shawnee, too?"

"Bill went to the Catholic school in South Shawnee. He's a year older than me. If you want to sit around and wait on him, I'm sure he'll be happy to talk over school days with you. He loves to rehash the old days."

"You don't?"

"No, I don't." She was getting really angry. With good reason, he supposed.

"Sorry, Mrs. Merrill. Sometimes I go overboard with questions." He reached in his pocket, pulled out a card, dropped it on the kitchen table. "If you think of anything, or if your father should say something now that I've disturbed him, there's my number. Call any time."

He made his exit through the back door and hurried around the corner of the house. He was halfway out the small alley when the gate swung open and a teenager came toward him. They exchanged hellos as they squeezed past each other.

Harter could feel the boy's questioning eyes on him as he pushed open the gate and walked through the archway to the Avenue.

··· 7 ···

Friday morning, one step inside the office, Harter glimpsed the pile of fresh messages on his desk and knew he had to do something. Things were only going to get worse for a while. The evening before, two of the three television networks had reported the strange case of a skeleton uncovered by the Killer Flood. NBC had even quoted Pete Epstein, which must have made the medical examiner's year. The story was big time now.

Instead of dropping into his chair, Harter turned and headed to the chief's office. His pitch was simple: If I've got to respond to all these goddamn calls and sort through old police reports, you can count on your only detective being tied up for a week or more. When he walked out of the chief's office fifteen minutes later, he had what he wanted. Harter usually got what he wanted.

The police should be sifting, Epstein had advised, and he was pretending to when Dave McManaway finally showed up. "I've commandeered you," said Harter, slamming a drawer shut on a filing cabinet.

"For what?"

Harter pointed over at his desk. "See all those notes. Every one of them is from someone who thinks they can identify the bones. You're going to be my sifter. You've been assigned to me for the duration."

"What you really need is a switchboard operator."

"Or a filing clerk."

"Would you have fixed it so Caruthers did this stuff?"

"If I could have. Look, you wanted to be a detective, didn't you? The door just swung open."

"Sally's not so sure."

"You mean she's not pregnant?"

McManaway laughed. "No, she's as pregnant as you can get. She's not sure about me being a detective. She thinks it's too dangerous, investigating murders and all."

"Hell, you're five times safer as a detective than as a beat cop. You're in more control of the situation. You've already been through the worst of it—years in a uniform, a sitting duck for any punk, ticketing cars when you don't know if the driver will pull a gun. You've been the first on a crime scene and had the anger vented right in your face. Tell Sally to stop worrying. Tell her you've got the chance to save your back. You won't have to dig skeletons out of the damn mud. Someone else'll be doing the hard labor. You'll just have to make sense of the bones once they're dug up. There's still plenty of mud involved, but most of it's mental work."

"'Mind Games.'"

"Huh?"

"'Mind Games.' It's an old John Lennon song."

"Was he a cop?" joked Harter.

"Not exactly."

Harter lit a cigarette and pointed to the piles of messages. "I've already done part of the sifting for you. Three stacks. This one is honest possibilities—women missing between Nineteen forty-five and, say, Nineteen seventy. At least that's what Epstein says. You'll notice it's the smallest bunch, only a few. The middle stack may be worth returning a call. The rest are probably meaningless, though you may want to keep an eye on them as things shape up."

McManaway nodded. "So, I'm to call about the honest possibilities, and maybe follow up on some of the others?"

"Yeah. And you'll no doubt be taking new calls as the day drags on. When you need a break from the phone—and you will—I want you to look through old police reports. If *Time* magazine calls, bluff them."

McManaway's green eyes registered confusion. "Bluff them? I've never done anything like this before."

"Who the hell has? You're smart enough to play it by ear. A detective never gets handed the sheet music."

"Damn, Harter. What old police reports am I supposed to hunt up?"

"A missing-persons report from about Nineteen forty-five, a Brenda Keith, Mrs. Paul Keith, who last lived on Fletcher Street. A hit-and-run death on Egypt Street in December Nineteen sixty-seven. Her name was—God, you believe I didn't get her first name? Look for a Wilton, Mrs. Wheat Wilton, maybe Mrs. Bartley W. Wilton. Can't have been many hit-and-runs in Shantytown in 'sixty-seven. While you're digging, see if you can find any files on women reported missing between Nineteen forty-five and Nineteen seventy, especially if there's a connection with South Shawnee."

"That's a long time. Twenty-five years," mumbled McManaway as he scribbled notes. "Were you a detective in Nineteen sixty-seven?"

"I was still a beat cop." *Mind games.* Harter had the feeling that working with McManaway was going to make him feel older than he usually did. "I want you to check the criminal records of some people, too. They're probably all clean, but I need to know who I'm dealing with."

McManaway picked up the pen again. "Shoot."

"Bartley Wheat Wilton and his wife, whatever her name was, and their son, Roger." Hell, he might as well have them all

46

checked out. "And their daughter, Dorothy Wilton Merrill, and Paul Keith and Brenda Harris Keith. And Matthew Curry. He's an old guy who lives across the street from the Wilton place. Want more to do?"

Before the younger cop could answer, the phone rang.

"Have a nice day," said Harter as he went out the door.

• • •

Outside, the assorted light breezes had congealed into a solid wind that made the signs overhanging the street twist on their chains like condemned men jerking now and then as if they'd been shot through with electrical current, like hanging wasn't good enough and the electric chair was needed to finish them off.

Kind, gentle Mother Nature again. At least the wind would dry up some of the mud.

He guessed it was in the midforties, but it seemed colder than when he'd come to work. He climbed in his car, turned the key, then settled back and stared out the windshield at the bare-branch trees shimmying on the mountains. Those Allegheny ridge lines surrounded Shawnee like the rim of a bowl. Sitting downtown, at the bottom, it was easy to imagine you were drowning in hot alphabet soup and the sides of the bowl were too slippery to climb out.

He'd told Liz those imaginings once, one night when they were in bed in the apartment over her dance studio, lying there, holding each other, looking out the open window at the mountain's shrouded, nighttime humps.

Liz. Damn.

He steered out of the lot, passed under the traffic light, then turned left onto the four-lane straight shot to the South Shawnee railroad complex. Past the Shawnee-Potomac shops

47

and the long scribbles of switchyard tracks, he turned left again, into the canal neighborhood.

A young fellow like you's got no notion how it was along the canal. Or so the old guy had claimed, the one who believed the bones belonged to his brother, Jimmy, the long-lost mule driver.

Actually, Harter did have some notion how it had been. Just as he'd grown up with tales of the 1936 Flood and the railroad's glory days when every passenger car was spit and polish, he'd heard stories of the Shawnee & Chesapeake Canal all of his life. Once, Shantytown had been winter quarters for many of the canalers. It had a reputation as a beat-your-head-in-for-a-buck place. He had no doubt there were moldy corpses to be dug up along the towpath. Even when he was a kid, South Shawnee had been full of taverns and aging roughnecks. Maybe Wheat Wilton and Matt Curry were among them.

Picturing Wilton frozen in his chair and Curry upset over the flood, it was hard to think of them as young and possibly violent men. But Dorothy Merrill had said, *Old men will feud.* What, he wondered, did they feud about?

He passed several large buildings on the lower side of the street. One of them could have been Darrell Phillips' warehouse, the warehouse that had been inundated Tuesday night, sending the appliance dealer into a deep depression. He guessed it didn't matter which of the buildings belonged to Phillips.

Just before turning up the hill to Fletcher Street, he noticed a street-cleaning truck coming toward him, spraying the silt and muck from the roadway, trying to wash it into the gutter.

One-thirteen Fletcher was a one-story shotgun house covered with smeary white aluminum siding. The place surely hadn't cost Paul and Brenda Keith much rent when they were newlyweds, and probably was even more of a bargain-basement residence now. When no one answered his knock, he tried next door.

The lady of the house was in her late forties. Her hugeness was displayed all too well by her tight lavender pants. Her hair was short and bobby-pinned flat.

"Got me," she said loudly in response to his questions. "Paul and Brenda Keith? Myrtle Harris? Never heard of none of them. Won't do you no good to come back and see that pair that lives next door, neither. They're just kids and don't know nothing from nothing. Ain't nobody on Fletcher Street lived here no longer than us. What do you need to know about these Keith people anyway? This got something to do with them bones they found down on Egypt Street? You out asking everyone?"

"Something like that," replied Harter.

"Well, you're talking forty years ago, before we even moved here."

Harter nodded and asked if she knew the Wiltons.

"Knew who they was. Had a girl and a boy, I think. That boy was always weird, like a beatnik. Remember when the mother was killed by a car or something. Don't know the details, but it certainly don't surprise me none they found a body down there."

"Why?"

"Why, the damn place is haunted. Everyone knows that. Sometimes you go by at night and you see white things moving inside."

"Lights?"

"Ghosts, if you ask me."

Harter visited three more houses before giving up. He should have known it would be hopeless to turn up much on a woman who'd lived there while her husband was in the service forty years before. Maybe Dave McManaway was having a better day, but he doubted it.

He drove down the hill and turned the corner onto Egypt

49

Street. Near the curb, waiting for the city garbage trucks, sat plastic trash bags, soggy overstuffed chairs, masses of pulp that had once been newspapers, magazines, books, family albums. Yards were filled with furniture, toys, boxes of stuff that people had carried out of their flooded basements.

He parked in front of the Wilton place, climbed out, and started back to where the bones had been uncovered. The hole was still there, roped off, surrounded by piles of dirt. He had the urge to walk up on the porch, force open the door, go in and face down what specters might show themselves. *White things moving inside.* Hell, he didn't believe in such crap. He hadn't spotted anything scary when he'd driven by on patrol late Wednesday night. And if there was ever a time for the house to show its haunters, it would have been Wednesday night, after the flood, after the bones had emerged, after the grave was disturbed. But the house had simply looked sad, wet, and deserted. Like a skeleton.

He let the notion pass. Going in the place would probably be as useless a gesture as the trip to Fletcher Street had turned out to be. No one had lived in the house for years, and the Wilton family had probably taken anything of value before trying to rent or sell it. Besides, it had been through the flood, so he'd just end up tramping around in a bog, and he'd done enough of that in the last two days. He wondered if the old floorboards would warp as they dried out, and what the Wiltons would do with the place now. Hard to make money off a flooded house with a bad reputation.

He turned away and began walking over to Matt Curry's. The night before, Curry's had been one of the few houses in Shantytown where lights had burned. Nearly everyone else had opted for warmth and dryness, but the old man was tough, not about to be frightened off by high water or howling demons.

He was ready to climb the steps to the retired conductor's

door when Spilky came up from the basement of the next house. Harter changed course and went over to see Curry's neighbor. "How's it going?"

"Could be better." Spilky dropped the box of jars he'd been toting. "We have to throw away all sorts of stuff. There's things you forget you have till you lose them. We canned these tomatoes in the summer. All that work, and now I wouldn't feel safe eating them. God knows what was in the floodwater."

"God might not even know," said Harter.

"Don't be sacrilegious, Detective." Spilky ran his mud-caked paw through his wiry hair. He didn't seem to notice—or simply didn't care—when some of the mud flaked off on top of his head.

"Is your wife over the upset of finding the bones?"

"Not entirely. It wasn't a pleasant thing to come across Wednesday morning, not on top of the flood. Have you made any progress?"

Progress. Strange choice of words, thought Harter. "We don't know much yet. Right now, I'm sort of digging into the past. Do you know any people who've lived around here a long time—people who might know about the Wiltons and others from years ago? Maybe they talk about Mrs. Wilton, who was killed in a hit-and-run, or about her son. Some other names have come up, too. I need someone who has forty years' worth of gossip."

"We're not acquainted with everyone, particularly the older folks. There's Mr. Curry, of course, but he'll change the subject if he doesn't like the question. We try to talk with him, but I always get the feeling we'll have to live here ten or fifteen years before he'll remember our names and talk about more than the weather. Some of these people are sure hard to get to know."

"Yeah," Harter agreed. "Sometimes people are hard to get to know."

51

... 8 ...

The air in the front room was chill, even though the furnace had been turned on that morning. The temperature was still in the fifties, and the house felt as damp as a barn on a rainy afternoon. Didn't smell any better than a barn, either. Matt Curry wondered if the cop was as bothered by the stench as he was.

Mennonite volunteers had helped him clean out the cellar on Thursday afternoon, but only a lot of long dry days would remove the terrible odor of the sewage-tinged floodwater mixed with fuel oil, rotting paper, and soaked fabric. Curry hoped he'd live long enough for the air to smell clean again.

God, his mother would have hated it. She'd been the sort who dusted and laundried every day. Cleanliness was next to godliness, and she'd wanted to be godly. She'd always called the front room the parlor, and had taken great pride in the furniture inherited from her family, and the neatly shelved books that had once belonged to her uncle, and the fussy curtains and doilies. Curry wasn't as fastidious. He'd stripped the room down to bachelor's quarters, putting most of the lace in a trunk . . . in a trunk downstairs . . . in a trunk that on Tuesday had floated in the foul mixture of destructive liquids. Sometimes, even after all the decades, he could still picture the front room—*the parlor*—as it had been when he was a boy.

"Damned if I remember Brenda Keith or her husband," he told Harter after the detective had worked from small talk to interrogation. "I do remember Myrtle Harris, and she did have a girl who lived with her, some relative she raised, but I can't help you there. Myrt Harris was a friend of my mother's. They were in the ladies group at the church and a couple times a year she'd come here to talk to Mother about church suppers or Bible study or something. She always seemed to be laughing. Never understood why. She hadn't had an easy life. Never had any money, never married, and then she had this girl dropped on her."

"So her niece never came with Miss Harris to visit your mother?"

"I don't know. I always tried to stay away from church goings-on. Mother had religion bad, and I disappeared when she got up a full head of steam. I told you how I got my name. She always wanted me to get an education and be a preacher like her uncle." Curry pointed to the bookshelves. "A lot of those books were his, at least the older, heavier ones. She was always after me to read them, and I was a smart kid, something of a reader, but what I read was Black Mask stories and things like Mark Twain. She never much approved. Like in *Huckleberry Finn*. You know that book? Miss Watson tried to save Huck's immortal soul—Mother used to speak of 'immortal souls'—and Huck wouldn't have any part of it. Neither would I. When we were growing up, Wheat Wilton and I used to pretend we were Huck Finn and Tom Sawyer, and that the Potomac was the Mississippi and the abandoned canal boats were our rafts. It disappointed Mother when I quit school and went to work for the Shawnee-Potomac, but times were hard after Dad ran off, and so when I was old enough I got a railroad job. Anyway, what do Myrt Harris and these Keith people have to do with anything?"

"Maybe nothing." Harter leaned back on the daybed and stared over at the old man in the worn, lumpy chair by the window. "Brenda Harris seems to have disappeared while her husband was in the service in World War Two."

"More than one woman did that, unfortunately."

"Did you ever marry, Mr. Curry?"

"No."

"Hell, I've probably asked too many questions about the Keiths already. Those names are running through the South Shawnee rumor mill by now."

"I won't help spread them. Not a hell of a lot of people ask me about anything anymore. I just don't recall the Keiths, and I told you my little connection with Myrt Harris. It's so long ago."

"I know. Believe me, I know. Can you think of anyone else who might help me?"

"Not as far as these people you're asking about. I should have told you before, though. Nan's younger brother still lives in town."

"Nan?"

"Nancy Wilton, Wheat's wife. We always called her Nan."

"And her brother lives in Shawnee?"

"Yeah. His name's David Nash, but we always called him Flathead. Lives up near the hospital," said Curry. "That's where Nan grew up, not down here in Shantytown. Flathead's in his fifties. He and Wheat never got along, so I don't know what he can tell you. I can't think of anyone else might know anything, but I'll keep chewing on it. I guess you've seen Wheat and his daughter. What'd they know?"

"Not much, I'm afraid. Wheat can't talk because of the stroke he had. Mostly he just sits in a chair. He did seem to react when I mentioned you, however. I guess you keep in touch with him."

"I don't know that I've seen him since he moved."

"Really?"

Curry tried not to show his hand, forced himself not to grab too hard at the arms of his understuffed chair. He didn't want Harter to believe there was bad blood between him and Wheat. He tried to sound disinterested when he asked, "How about Dorothy?"

"She claimed to have no ideas about the bones. She did say you and your old friend sure could argue."

Curry tried to be careful. "Maybe we knew each other too good."

"That's how she put it. Did you fellows have particular topics of debate?"

"I'm sure we did. Politics, the best makes of cars—of course, I don't have a car anymore. Can't afford it."

"What about the son, Roger? I'd like to track him down. You remember him?"

"Well, he grew up across the street."

"Dorothy Merrill seems angry about him. Could just be that he's left her with full responsibility for their father, but I sensed it ran deeper."

"All families have their ins and outs."

"What do you mean?"

"I mean, Dorothy was always close to Wheat, like girls will be to fathers. If you've seen her, you know she took after Wheat in looks and temperament. Roger was more like Nan, with dark hair and fine features. She was a good-looking woman, Nan, and she had a hot streak that could flare up."

"Did Roger inherit the temper, too?"

"As I remember, he did. Like Nan—"

"What?"

"Once she and Wheat had a little argument in the kitchen when she was doing dishes . . . Wheat told me about it later . . . She had a carving knife in her hand, and she just threw it at him. Damn thing stuck in the wall a foot from his head. No, sir, you didn't want to make that woman mad, I'll tell you. Other times, she'd be so jolly she'd break into a jig when some song came on the radio, and you'd think she was the May Queen. Her emotions always ran strong, one way or another."

"And so did Roger's?"

"Never heard of him throwing knives, if that's what you're asking. But you never could tell what he'd do. Totally unpredictable boy. Not that he wasn't smart, mind you. Nan was always sharper than Wheat, and like I said, the boy took after her in all ways. She spoiled him tremendous. Presents at Christmas they couldn't really afford. A car when he got out of high school. She said that was so he could travel to college, but he could have taken the bus. I know Wheat and Nan had it out plenty of times over Roger. But Nan could never see anything bad about the boy. She'd always find an excuse for him."

"And Wheat didn't?"

"No."

"Could that be why the boy left home after his mother died?"

"Could be. I'm sure Wheat made it hot for him. He wouldn't put up with half the shenanigans Nan would. I remember once he blew his stack when he and Nan came home from being out of town and some of the neighbors complained about a crazy party Roger had thrown with loud music and girls screaming."

"You remember any of his friends?"

"Never paid much attention. I suppose they were from the college."

"He went to the community college, didn't he?"

"That's what he was supposed to be doing, but from what I heard, he was pretty spotty about going to class and kept dropping in and out of school. I think he used the college mostly as a place to hang out. Nan really got on him about it, but with her, she might yell and even throw a knife, but then it was out of her system, and the next day it was all done and forgotten. I believe she'd have left Wheat before she left that boy."

"Wheat and she had problems?"

Curry sat silently for a full minute, then said, "I don't know. I didn't live with them."

"You remember when she was killed?"

"Yeah. It was December Nineteen sixty-seven. Sleeted the night before and Egypt Street was all ice. Some guy going to work saw the body and almost wrecked his car when he hit his brakes and tried to stop on the ice. The police seemed to think that whoever it was hit her did the same thing. Lost control, and was too afraid to stop."

"Who was the investigating officer?"

Curry shrugged. "Average-size guy with light skin and light brown hair. He came around and asked questions, like you're doing, but I never saw him again."

"Caruthers," mumbled Harter. Then he realized the name would mean nothing to the old man. "Why would Nan Wilton have been out in the street on such a nasty night?"

"You keep asking me things I can't answer. I'm not the Wise Old Man of the Mountains."

"I guess Wheat took it hard."

"Of course he did. He'd worked the night it happened and showed up home when they were moving her body. It was a tough way to find out."

"And the boy?"

"Broke up."

Harter seemed to be waiting for him to say something else,

but Curry just waited, too. Finally, the detective asked, "Do you have any new thoughts about the bones?"

"Not a clue."

"We're almost in the same boat," said Harter, pushing himself up from the sofa. "Mind if I use your phone before I go? It is working, isn't it?"

"They fixed the lines a couple hours ago. Go back through that door to the kitchen. It's on the wall."

Once the cop had left the room, Curry climbed to his feet and stepped as lightly as he could to the far end of the room. His hearing wasn't what it used to be, and at first he couldn't make out more than a few words. Then either he tuned in or Harter's voice got louder.

The detective was obviously talking to someone at police headquarters. He told the other cop that Mrs. Wilton's name had been Nancy, then asked what had come to light. After that, Harter fell into a series of yeah's and no's. The conversation ended so abruptly that Curry was stranded like a buck dancer in the middle of a sawdust floor when the cop returned to the front room.

He knew Harter knew he'd been eavesdropping, but nothing was said.

... 9 ...

Curry turned down the burner under the skillet so the fresh side didn't burn. *Fresh side.* Most kids didn't even know what it was anymore, but he'd grown up with it. Hard to imagine now, but once many of the families in Shantytown had raised pigs and chickens. Stys and coops had stood in backyards, and each fall they had slaughtered hogs.

He'd always liked fresh side better than bacon. Hard to find the stuff now. The city had an ordinance against livestock within the limits, and the meat in supermarkets came from big packing plants, not from local farmers. Young people probably believed those plastic-wrapped chickens were manufactured in Japan. Only a small butcher shop near the railroad shops still sold fresh side, and then only occasionally.

He scooped the strips of pork onto the soft bread and remembered helping his mother cut the head off a chicken. He usually held the bird by its legs as she wielded the axe. The thing's head was outstretched, resting on a stump in the backyard, and the axe had fallen, neatly severing the neck. For a short time the body would squirm and the wings would flap madly. Always amazed him the chicken didn't know it was dead.

59

The first time he'd swung the axe, he'd botched it. He'd missed, or rather he hadn't hit it square on. The blade had just nicked the bird's neck, and blood squirted everywhere. The chicken, a strong, fat, Sunday dinner one, had battled to get free, its head half cut off. "Hit it again! You can't do that!" his mother was screaming. "Don't make it suffer! When you kill something, do it fast!"

He swung the axe again.

The coop was gone now.

Sometimes it seemed like everything was gone now. Like the passenger station. *A museum.* Earlier, as they'd small-talked, before the detective had launched into heavy questions, Harter had asked if he was going to the opening of the museum on Saturday. Curry had said he didn't know. But later, talking to Flathead, he'd decided maybe he would.

He'd tried to call Flathead Nash, Nan's brother, for hours. Flathead had been a Marine, and when he'd come home from the service, he'd continued to wear his hair sheared into a crew cut. This had been in the 1950s, when many schoolboys wore waxed crew cuts. One day Flathead had taken his nephew Roger to the barbershop and delivered him home with only stubble left on top. Nan had gone wild. If she'd been washing a butcher knife that afternoon, she would have thrown it. And if she'd wanted to, she would have hit Flathead, too, just as she could have hit Wheat, if she'd really wanted to.

But Flathead didn't answer any of Curry's calls. He was probably sitting in a tavern somewhere. Curry wondered if Harter would have the same trouble locating him. He hoped so. He wanted to talk to Nash before the detective did.

After he washed his dinner dishes, he dialed Nash's number again. Flathead had a voice as thick as his bull neck, and Curry was relieved when he heard it. No, Flathead didn't want to drive to Shantytown this evening. He had to be careful. He was a little drunk, and if they picked him up one more time, he might lose his license for good. But, yeah, he'd come by in the morning and they'd go to the museum opening. No, he hadn't talked to no detective yet. He'd been away all afternoon. After hearing about the bones, he'd visited Wheat, but it was impossible to communicate with the son of a bitch. Wheat just stared out the window. Then Flathead had gone for a few beers to think things through. He'd been intending to call Curry.

After he hung up, Curry went to the parlor and sat in his chair. The house still smelled like a big rat had died in the woodwork, but he tried to ignore the stench. He twisted and peered across Egypt Street at the Wilton place. There he was. In his chair. Staring out the window. Like they said Wheat Wilton did, the son of a bitch.

Everything was being kicked loose. Like rocks tumbling down a mountain.

When he and Wheat were young, they'd often played on a hillside above the tracks. There'd been an old wives' tale that a penny was all you needed to derail a train, so he and Wheat, *Huck and Tom*, had of course tried it. They'd put a copper coin on a rail, then scrambled up the shale bank until a freight came along. The train didn't leave the tracks. After it had passed, they couldn't even find the penny.

Later, as a conductor, he remembered their attempt many times. *What if the copper sliver had caused the wheels to skip connection with the rail and wreck the train?* When he saw boys sitting on rocky ridges along the line, he never failed to wonder if they too laid pennies on the tracks.

Sometimes those kids scrambled up a shale bank like he and Wheat once had, and their scurrying caused rocks to come unstuck, and the rocks skittered down the hill toward the train. Seemed to him that, other times, those rocks came loose of their own accord, just popped out of their rightful places on the hillsides. Like on those mountain roads where the signs warn FALLING ROCK. As if there was something you could do about it. Rocks falling. Coming unstuck. Someone had either kicked them free in a scramble, or the rocks loosened themselves at some predestined moment. Could cause a car to swerve out of control. Could derail a train. Could kill someone. *If you kill something, do it fast!*

She'd been lying in the middle of Egypt Street that icy morning, 1967. Just wearing her slippers and her pink robe, open to show her underclothes and her thighs.

Unbelievable, that it had happened. Unbelievable, that he hadn't heard a sound, not a collision, not a scream of brakes, not a yell of pain. He'd always felt guilty about it. If he'd only heard something, he might have run outside and saved her. Might have called an ambulance. Might have gotten her to the hospital while she was still breathing.

She'd only been crossing the street. She shouldn't have been in danger.

Now she was wearing a dress so thin you could see her body move through it, the soft kind of dress the girls wore before the war, with shiny stockings and high-heel shoes that strapped across her slender ankles.

Curry had been heading home from work when he first laid eyes on her that warm day in 1941. She was new to him, not from Shantytown or even South Shawnee, and she was waiting for the bus to take her home. He passed her day after day, until he built up enough nerve to speak to her. It took months.

She was a secretary in the union office near the Shawnee-Potomac shops. Once he learned that, he pretended he had reason to go in the office frequently, just to see her. Finally he asked her to go to the movies with him, and she said yes. Nan smelled so clean as she sat in the theater seat next to him.

"Did you ever marry, Mr. Curry?" the detective had inquired.

"No."

She married Wheat Wilton, who always seemed to know what to say to the girls.

Unsure of himself, Curry's tongue had balled up whenever he was near a good-looker like Nan, but Wheat was glib as hell. Never had a problem. *Funny.* Now he was the old man who rattled on, and golden-throated Wheat had been struck dumb.

He'd known the night he saw Nan with Wheat at the ticket window that he'd lost her. Wheat, always light and joking with the girls. Curry had retreated around the corner and gone home. After that, when he'd pass her at the bus stop, he couldn't manage more than "Hello." He was afraid to ask her out and be turned down. Didn't want to hear her say, "I'm sorry, but I'm going with Wheat."

They married in the summer of 1943 and moved into the house across the street. Soon after, Wheat's mother went to live with her sister and they had the house to themselves. From his window, Curry would watch Nan as she hung laundry out back or sat on the front porch. Her belly swelled, and seven months after the wedding, Dorothy was born.

He hadn't been surprised that Wheat had taken her away from him. Wheat always got what he wanted. What surprised Curry came later.

She'd only been crossing the street. She shouldn't have been in danger.

... 10 ...

Harter shifted in the booth and watched Al load a couple dozen of those pencil-thin hot dogs onto the cooker rollers inside the big front window, where the rotating wieners could be seen from the sidewalk. Al called that advertising.

Despite the early hour, Al's regulars were already filling the stools at the Formica counter and calling for hot dogs with the works. When business boomed at midday, Al would be so swamped that he'd line eight or nine buns up his tattooed arm and, assembly line style, slip the franks inside, then slop mustard on each with a flat stick, then spoon on diced onions, then cover it all with his secret-recipe chili.

Weenies, Harter's grandfather had called them, and that first Edward Harter had always ordered hamburgers—*hamburgs*—instead. Family tradition held that his grandfather's aversion to hot dogs stemmed from a pre–World War I visit to a railroad exposition or some such event in Chicago or some other city Midwest, where he'd gotten food poisoning from bad weenies in those days of unregulated meat.

Harter had more than enough dreads, but hot dogs weren't among them, no matter what the health food people warned. He could almost qualify as one of Al's regulars. Many a morning he'd eaten those wieners for breakfast, though usually, like this Saturday, he settled for coffee. Breakfast—a big victual feast of country sausage, yellow-yoke eggs, crisp hash browns, buttered toast—was his favorite meal, even if he was more likely to down it at 2 A.M. in the old diner by the South Shawnee yards than at a more orthodox time.

He lit a cigarette and stared at the local page of *The News*. At least the paper had backed off on the Egypt Street bones, though he guessed the story would be back on top once Pete Epstein and his expert were ready to say something.

The flood didn't earn much newspaper space, either. It had only been four days, and the victims were still trying to put their worlds in shape, but the sole mention of the disaster was a photo of Mennonite volunteers helping a Shantytown family, as they had helped Matt Curry. Crews of Mennonites had simply come out of the woodwork the day after the flood and gone quietly about their business, washing down walls, trucking away ruined goods, replacing warped doors, doing anything to make life easier for people. Where those peaceful folks lived between tragedies, Harter didn't know, but he did know his job would be a whole lot less complicated if everyone had their sense of moral duty.

What *The News* blasted across the headlines was the opening of the railroad museum. There had been talk of postponing the event in the wake of the flood, but the project was already running late. The one hundredth birthday of the old Shawnee-Potomac station had been in June, and it was now November. If they didn't cut the ribbon, the year would slip by, or at least bad weather would come and there would be fewer tourists. *Tourists*. Somehow Harter didn't believe they would satisfactorily replace steel mills and railroad shops. In a way, turning the passenger station into a museum marked its demise, too, though he was glad the building still stood.

65

He could see the top floor of the station from his third-floor apartment on the hill. He'd grown up near the enormous structure, which in its heyday had had hotel rooms on its second and third stories. When he and his friends could find nowhere else to play, when they were tired of skinned-up knees from sliding into third base in gravel yards and alleys, they had sometimes sneaked over the wrought-iron fence into the green field near the station and used it for a ball diamond until the railroad bulls came to run them off.

Like many Shawnee residents, he'd felt like an aged relative was dying when, a few years before, they'd talked of tearing the station down. This had been in 1982, during the depths of the recession, and the building had long since become little more than a holding zone for freight. Even when he'd been a kid, he'd heard how the upper hotel floors were rotting. The station's death seemed to represent everything that was going wrong.

Now the Governor, a U.S. Senator, a Congressman, and scores of state legislators and local officials were to cut the museum ribbon and announce a bright new day. The chief was worried about security, so Harter had promised he'd mix in the crowd as long as the dignitaries stayed around.

Hell, he'd have gone anyway. He'd asked Liz to come along, but she hadn't shown any interest. The distance between them just kept widening, and there didn't seem to be anything he could do about it. Besides, she had her Saturday morning dance classes to teach. He didn't want to think about it. There was enough going on to pull him down without dwelling on Liz.

"Manage to get some sleep last night?"

He looked up to see Dave McManaway. "What?"

"Did you get a good night's sleep? I figured you could use it."

"I always sleep the same, good or bad."

McManaway had no sooner sat down than Al put a cup of

coffee on the Formica tabletop in front of him. As he watched the younger cop spoon some sugar into the cup, Harter had a flash of what Al's was like when he was little, when there were scratched-up wood tables, not the smooth Formica mandated by the health department. Why was he rolling and tumbling through the past? Always rolling and tumbling through the past. The old wooden tables. His grandfather's distaste for weenies. The 1936 Flood. The station. The bones surfacing. All coming up like water from underground pipes.

"I waited until after five yesterday," said McManaway, "but you didn't come back to the office. I imagine you had a full day on the case."

"Full enough. Actually, I stopped in at headquarters last night. I saw the stuff you dug out and read some of the messages. Good job."

He didn't bother to tell McManaway that, unable to find Nan Wilton's brother, he'd driven out to the overlook on the mountain south of Shawnee and just killed time. How many hours had he wasted over the years, simply sitting in his car and looking down on the model train—layout city he was supposed to be protecting?

"Then you saw Caruthers' accident report from Nineteen sixty-seven?"

"Yeah. I figured Caruthers was the investigating officer."

"He doesn't seem to have turned up much. Apparently he questioned a lot of people in the neighborhood and measured tire skids and all, but no one was ever charged. He believed it was a pickup truck, probably blue, based on a paint smear on Nan Wilton's robe. Caruthers didn't really say much about it. In general, he kept good notes, though."

"He always did. Even back when you didn't have to do half the paperwork we do now. He was a red-tape specialist. I used to tell him he'd make a great federal bureaucrat." Harter pulled his cigarette pack from his jacket and shook out a smoke.

"There's something to be said for good record keeping when you're digging into an accident that happened eighteen years ago," McManaway said.

"Guess so."

"What did you find out about these Keith people?"

"Nothing much. Nobody really remembers them. I sort of decided to put the whole thing on hold until I hear from Pete Epstein. No sense banging my brains out until we know more about the bones."

"Dr. Epstein's promised something this afternoon?"

"Yeah. I plan to stop at his office after I work crowd control at the museum opening. You going to it?"

"Never thought about it. No one asked me. I promised I'd take Sally shopping this afternoon. We're working on the baby's room. It's due in ten days."

Harter rubbed out his cigarette on the lip of the green glass ashtray, then reached for his coffee. "How'd *your* day go yesterday?"

"Well, I had a lot of callers, but not as many as you had on Thursday. Could be cooling down. I can't say there were any true leads. Confused people, aren't they? We could hand the girl's name, age, address, and photo to the papers and we'd still hear from people who claim, no, it's not her at all, it's really my great-great-grandfather, who had a long gray beard and rode a big white horse. Hard to believe so many men and women have just up and disappeared without a trace, and that someone out there still wants to find out what became of them."

"Yeah. It's enough to make you as cynical as me. I didn't start out that way, you know."

"As far as those names you left me, I can't find a criminal record for any of them. I'm not saying there's nothing, but I just haven't found it. I put out requests for the whereabouts of your Roger Wilton, but it's a huge country."

"Anything else going on?"

"Usual Friday night crap. Herr says there was a bad accident out on the interstate, and a burglary reported on the West Side, not far from where Liz lives, actually. A drunk highway worker drove into a drainway at three A.M. and claimed he was checking culverts. A sixteen-year-old kid rammed his hand through a plate glass window downtown and set off the alarm. When Bettles showed up, the kid was frozen in place, high on something, watching the blood run down his arm."

"Friday night crap, all right. Be sure and tell Sally all the gory details. Let her know that, as a detective, you won't have to deal with half that garbage."

"Yeah, but they're cut-and-dried cases, mostly. How do you even start to figure out who killed someone when all you've got is a few old bones?"

"Why do I have to keep reminding everyone that we don't know for sure whether anybody killed anybody?" said Harter. "But as for learning what happened, I sure as hell don't know how to go about it. I'm not the Wise Old Man of the Mountains."

… **11** …

Politicians sure could talk.

Carpenters hammered, writers wrote, cabdrivers drove, engineers engineered, plumbers piped, mechanics tinkered, cops investigated, dancers danced, and politicians talked.

Harter was beginning to wonder when the hell they'd ever cut the damn ribbon. In their dark suits, they sat on the long, broad porch of the passenger station. One by one, they rose from their folding chairs and, amid applause, strutted to the podium. There was a definite pecking order. The Mayor kicked off the show with a welcome, and then the county commissioners waved and said a few words, and then the state legislators got a few minutes to explain their role in saving the old station and boosting tourism, and then came Congressman Charles Whitford Canley, who apparently had the office for life.

Whether anybody was really listening to all the glowing words was beside the point. Harter knew that what the politicians truly wanted was to be seen by voters, to make it look like they were doing something to improve the lives of ordinary people. They really wanted Jack Reese or one of the other camera-aimers to snap their pictures so they might end up on the front page Sunday morning.

Reese was a photographer for *The News*. A few years before, his angular shots had convinced everyone that the station was a monument worth saving. Now he and others pointed their cameras at the politicians on the porch. There were also television news crews from Bartlesburg, even from Washington and Baltimore. The Governor and the U.S. Senator had brought along their own photographers so they could remind voters that their benevolent realms did indeed encompass Shawnee.

The crowd of four or five hundred was turning bored long before the climax. Amid the babble of politicians, the only real puzzle was whether the Governor or the Senator would speak first, or rather last. Who would get star billing?

A sizable chunk of those gathered on the station platform were old men who, Harter imagined, had once worked for the Shawnee-Potomac. But even they could stand only so much talk of the importance of the railroad to the development of the state and region, and how the museum commemorated the industry while at the same time it opened the door for a new industry, tourism, which would again bring good days. The old men shifted from foot to foot and at times would have drowned out the speakers if the public-address system hadn't been turned up loud.

The Governor got the final word. He had the good taste to inform the crowd that he and the Senator planned to tour the flood-ravaged sections in the afternoon, and that they were hard at work trying to get President Reagan to declare the region a federal disaster area. Harter wondered if, like the Mennonites, the politicos would help clear the mud away. Or would they helicopter off after an hour or so?

Finally, the speeches were over and the politicians all

clumped near the red ribbon. Two pairs of oversize scissors were produced, and as the Governor and the Senator clipped, the photographers clicked. Then, accompanied by a couple of state troopers, the dignitaries filed inside for a look at what they had christened.

Harter didn't rush in. He stood on the platform awhile, watching everyone. Without doubt, this was the most activity that had taken place there in thirty years. Even his cynicism couldn't erase that fact. He was glad they hadn't torn the station down. Hell, he just might vote for the Governor himself.

He'd about fallen into a daydream about the old building when he saw the short, stocky old man climb the steps and walk across the porch toward the double doors, over which now hung the sign SHAWNEE RAILROAD MUSEUM. There was something familiar about the man, but at first Harter didn't register it was the same fellow he'd spent so much time with in the last few days.

Only when the man turned to open the door did Harter recognize Matt Curry, dressed in his best. The dark brown suit was a little rumpled in back, but still you could have believed he was one of the special guests. Beside him was a guy in his fifties who hadn't bothered to deck out for the occasion, wearing instead blue corduroy trousers, a faded plaid flannel shirt, and a light gray jacket.

The Governor and his entourage were already leaving as Harter went up the steps. Inside the doors, other politicians congregated to shake the hands of those who came and went. Harter brushed by them and made his way to the center of the tile floor. All around him, people chattered as they studied the railroad exhibits. A man dressed in a Shawnee-Potomac conductor's blue uniform stood behind what had once been the ticket counter. Above his head was a sign that read TOURIST INFORMATION.

They'd done a great job fixing the place up. The freshly painted walls probably hadn't looked so good since World War II. The enormous waiting room, now filled with bodies and echoing with voices, didn't seem anywhere near as dingy and run-down as it had the last time he'd been in it.

He found himself gravitating to the souvenir machine near the counter, *the information desk*. The contraption was still there. They'd even shined it up. In the old days, you slid a quarter in the slot and turned a wheel to find each letter of your name, or whatever message you wanted to press into metal. Apparently the machine still worked, though the price had been upped to a buck. In a drawer somewhere he still had one of those thin, silvery disks with his name and birth date embossed on it.

Across the room, a huge, colorful map hung on the wall, and standing in front of it were Matt Curry and the other man. Harter moved over to them, but they seemed so entranced by the map that they didn't realize he was standing behind them.

"The domain of the Shawnee-Potomac Railroad, huh?" he eventually asked to seize their attention.

"Yeah," mumbled Curry, who didn't seem too surprised at Harter's sudden appearance. The seventy-year-old reached up and almost touched the plastic-coated map with his thick index finger. "I know all the damn stops. I spent a quarter of my life calling them out as I went through the cars punching tickets. *North Branch, Green Spring, Paw Paw, Doe Gully, Hancock, Cherry Run, Martinsburg, Shenandoah Junction, Harpers Ferry, Brunswick, Point of Rocks, Germantown, Rockville, Kensington, Washington, D.C.* Most of them were littler towns then, you understand. Hell, the Shawnee-Potomac was littler, too. Wasn't part of some national conglomerate in those days, but it was a tremendous thing to those of us who worked for it. We believed it was the most important company in the world. Anyway, we'd be steaming along and I'd call out those stops, then head back to the caboose and sip my coffee and read. Others might have drank, but I read to bide the time. They used to call me the Professor, did I tell you that?"

"I don't think so," said Harter, watching Curry closely. The brown suit didn't look as dapper as it had at a distance. Far from new, it had wide lapels and a sort of old-fashioned cut. It made the old man look hardy and barrel-chested. Such suits were back in style, Liz had told him one night, and she'd suggested he might try one. *Maybe he should have.*

"*Washington, D.C., Kensington, Rockville . . .*" Curry was running the return route west now. Harter remembered all the stops, too. His grandfather had been given a railroad pass when he'd retired, and as long as Harter was under twelve, the two of them could ride anywhere on the Shawnee-Potomac for free. Once, with a chicken box lunch, they'd traveled to Washington to see the inauguration of Dwight D. Eisenhower. "*. . . Green Spring, North Branch . . .*"

"Brings back a lot," said the man with Curry. "I'm not sure I want it all to come back. Where's the pictures of the damn wrecks, or don't they put them on display?"

"They're probably tucked in a dark corner someplace," said Harter. "I don't think I know you."

"Flathead Nash," answered the guy without extending his hand. "I don't know you, neither."

"This is the detective I told you about," Curry told him. Turning to Harter, he added, "This is David Nash, Nan's brother."

"I tried to find you yesterday," Harter said.

"I'm tough to find sometimes." Nash's voice had turned gruffer. Harter guessed he didn't like cops.

"I guess Mr. Curry's told you what I'm interested in."

"Yeah."

"I know this isn't the time, but I want to come by and ask you some questions."

"Well, you can ask." Flathead Nash had a blotchy red face and all the finesse of a drunken rowdy.

"Suppose I come up to your house Monday morning. Right now, I'm waiting for a report on the bones they found at the Wilton place. Once I get it, I may have a clearer idea what I need to find out," said Harter.

"I don't know a goddamn thing about no bones. Matt says you've been asking about Nan's accident, too. I wasn't even in town when it happened. She and Wheat led their life and I led mine."

"How about your nephew, Roger Wilton? I've been trying to locate him."

"Ain't seen the boy in almost twenty years, not since he left home."

"You just collect your thoughts. I'll be around Monday."

"My thoughts are collected, and I ain't got none," barked Nash.

Maybe he's telling the truth, thought Harter. Maybe he ain't got no thoughts. Not wanting to push it at the moment, he said his good-byes and backed away from them.

As he walked toward the door, he noticed the crowd had thinned out considerably. Only one or two politicians still worked the station. There didn't seem to be many tourists that November day.

··· 12 ···

Turning onto the street above the station, Harter could see across the downtown to the opposite hill where a steeple pierced the sky. Pete Epstein's office was only a few doors from the old church, but getting from the station to the steeple was something else again. Shawnee hadn't been designed for modern traffic. By the time you allowed parking on the hilly streets, the actual driving space was pretty narrow.

Harter couldn't remember whether it had been worse in the 1950s when cars were wider and longer, but it sure was a mess now. Some high-priced traffic engineer had changed half the streets into one-way affairs. Then, in the 1970s, to create a mall atmosphere, they'd bricked in the main downtown street and diverted all cars and trucks around it. The result lent credence to what the old man on a country road once said: *You can't get there from here.*

As the crow flies, it was possibly three-quarters of a mile to the medical examiner's, but to drive it he had to turn up the hill behind the station, go three blocks, turn up another hill by the YMCA, curve around a corner, ease into southbound traffic heading back the way he'd come, wait at the crossing for a freight to pass, then bump over the tracks, turn left, then right twice, then eventually left again, and, near the flood-control walls, cross the river bridge from his own East End into the more well-to-do West Side where he roared up the hill until he came to the Episcopal Church. Luckily, Pete Epstein had a private parking lot, so he didn't have to sniff around for a spot on the street.

He stubbed out his cigarette, climbed from the car, and decided to try the small brick building where Epstein did his police work, rather than the office where he doctored his regular patients.

Epstein was smiling like he knew something when Harter walked in. "Good, you're early," he said. "I might be able to get home and watch a football game yet."

"Where's your expert?" asked Harter.

"Probably on his way back to the university. We worked on the bones a few hours last night after Dr. Shaw got into town. Then this morning we really went at it. Come on back. I'll show you what we've got."

Epstein's short, wiry body almost leaped from the chair. He led Harter through the door to the autopsy room, a room the detective had seen more than once. Spread atop thin white paper on the table were the beige bones, now washed and sorted. When he'd seen them three days before in Wilton's backyard, Harter had found it hard to feel anything, to even accept that they were the remains of a person. Maybe it was because of all the phone calls, especially the one from Paul Keith about his late wife, Brenda, or maybe it was because the bones were now laid out into a skeleton, but he no longer had trouble acknowledging that they had once been a breathing person.

"What we've got is a young woman, like I thought," Epstein began.

"How young?"

"Twenty, twenty-one. It's easier to pinpoint the age with kids."

"How long ago was she buried?"

"We decided it must have been around Nineteen sixty-six, though it could have just as well been anywhere from, say, 'sixty-four to 'sixty-eight. Slightly unusual conditions, you understand. On the one hand, she was buried in the shed, a sheltered area, and on the other, the body was in the floodplain along the river. Given all the variables, it's hard to be much more exact. We don't believe there's any reason to doubt she was buried there shortly after she died."

"You're positive this happened in the sixties, and not Nineteen forty-five?" asked Harter, thinking again of Brenda Keith.

"There's no way we're that far off. I wouldn't want to mislead you by being so specific that you rule out real possibilities, but, no, it couldn't have been forty years ago. Dr. Shaw took a few bones back with him, so we might hear more from him in the next two or three weeks. All I can do is help you calculate your probabilities."

"Any idea how she died?"

Epstein ran his hand through his gray hair. "Got me. No broken bones. No evidence of a knife wound or a bullet, though unless they hit a bone, there wouldn't have to be. She could have been strangled, or smothered, or she could have even died from natural causes."

"At twenty?"

Epstein shrugged. "I'll admit it's unlikely. The bones suggest she was about five-six, healthy, and probably slim, though again, that's a guess. People can put fat on thin frames."

"How about dental records? You mentioned them to the press."

"They just picked up on that. Dental records are a shell game. You have to have some notion who the victim is. You can't just send X rays to every dentist in the United States and expect them to go back and match them against their old files. Dental records only verify. Some dentists aren't good about keeping old charts, and since we're talking twenty years ago, there's no assurance the dentist is still in practice, or even alive. Still, her teeth were well taken care of. They were fluoridated at some point, which was often done to kids in the fifties. We did find one new thing."

"What's that?"

Epstein turned to a white metal cabinet, picked something up, and handed it over to Harter. "I took Dr. Shaw out to Egypt Street this morning so he could have a look at the scene and the soil and everything. He sifted a little and came up with this earring. I guess we were too busy hunting for bones the other day and, with the mud and all, just missed it."

"Doesn't look that unusual. Plenty of women have pierced ears. Hell, it could have belonged to Nan Wilton, or been dropped anytime over the years."

"Sure could have," said Epstein. "But it's still something. Besides, I'm not sure as many girls had pierced ears twenty or twenty-five years ago. I remember when my daughter had hers done. It was a big deal, and we gave her hell when she came home. Besides, that's not a dime-store earring. The little half-moon is ivory, I think. Isn't much, but it's yours now."

"Any other big insights?" asked Harter as he stuffed the earring into his jacket pocket.

"Not right now. All we can do is hope to hear more from Dr. Shaw. You'll be glad to know, Harter, that so far I've resisted the temptation to inform the media. They keep calling, but I just let them talk to my answering machine."

"My God, Pete, when did you see the light? Hell, I might vote for you yet, once you decide what you're running for."

Christ, he thought. First the Governor, and now Pete Epstein. If this day dragged on much longer, he'd have promised his votes for the rest of his life.

● ● ●

As soon as he reached headquarters, Harter dug through the notes on his desk, found Paul Keith's number in Pittsburgh, and dialed it. A woman answered, and he was relieved she didn't ask who he was when he asked for Keith.

Once Keith was on the line, Harter got straight to the point. The bones couldn't have been Brenda's. There was little or no doubt they were from the 1960s. Of course, it didn't help Keith understand what had become of his first wife, but at least it didn't open a closet of skeletons, and anyway, the old man had long lived without knowing about her. Perhaps it was best that way.

What bothered Harter was how much time he'd wasted on the trail of the 1940s disappearance. *Mind games*, like Dave McManaway would say. He'd spent Friday questioning people about the Keiths, and as he'd told Matt Curry, he'd probably stoked the rumor fires in South Shawnee. He knew too well how rumors could burn through blue-collar neighborhoods. Were upper-crust neighborhoods any different?

Still, he had gotten to know Curry, and had visited the Wiltons, and had finally met Flathead Nash, Nan's brother, and had soaked in a lot of Shantytown. No matter what, the body had been buried in a shed behind the Wilton house. Someone had to know something. Someone had to have something to do with it.

He reached in his pocket, pulled out the earring, and fingered the ivory half-moon. Liz had pierced ears. Maybe he'd see her tonight. Then he dropped the earring and tried to drop the thought as he began reading the messages on his desk.

80

McManaway had meticulously jotted down the remarks of each caller and how they related, or didn't relate, to the bones. Clearly, he was better educated than the cops of Harter's generation or the ones who had trained him.

Suddenly he saw an older detective rambling on to a young one, and he was the young one, 1968.

"First thing you got to learn, Harter, is anything can happen. Don't think just because you're in a small city in the mountains don't mean that all the big-city crimes don't rear their heads. They just don't pop up as often, which can make them trickier, since you don't always know how to solve them. Don't ever let your guard down. Anything that can happen in New York or Los Angeles can happen here. *Anything.*"

Hell, the molemen could come tomorrow.

The telephone rang.

"Are you the one investigating the bones?"

The man's voice was unaccented and bland, like he was enunciating clearly and slowly to cover up his real voice.

"Yeah."

"I would like to talk to you."

"We're talking."

"No. I mean in person."

"I'm at headquarters now, or I could meet you somewhere."

"Not right now. I have things I have to do. Tonight. Somewhere no one will see us. Not there."

"Who are you?" asked Harter.

"Not right now."

"Where are you?"

"Not important. Name a place to meet."

"How about the old Shawnee-Potomac station?" asked Harter, the museum opening still fresh in his mind. "By the pedestrian underpass. There shouldn't be anyone there this evening."

"After dark."
"Eight o'clock."
"Make it eleven."
The line went dead.
The old cop was right.
Eleven o'clock at the station.
Anything can happen.

··· 13 ···

"So if Dr. Epstein's right, and the bones are from between Nine-teen sixty-four and Nineteen sixty-eight, we're looking at almost the same time frame as the hit-and-run case you had me dig out," said Dave McManaway.

Harter rubbed his palms against the steering wheel. "Yeah, I guess we are, but don't jump to the conclusion they're con-nected in any way. They could be years apart."

"All of Caruthers' paperwork might help you yet."

"Let's hope he didn't toil in vain."

"You know, this is just the sort of thing Sally's worried about. I mean, us here, tonight, sitting in an unmarked car in the shadows of an empty parking lot, you preparing to step out and come face to face with someone who wouldn't even give you his name."

"That's the breaks," Harter said. "Didn't you ever patrol the station platform on your beat?"

"Yeah, but—"

"But nothing. We've been through all that. Anyway, I've done dumber things. Besides, I wasn't so damn stupid. I brought you along, didn't I? Keep your window down and your ears sharp. If anyone jumps me, I'll raise a hell of a fuss. I'll get off a shot or two if I need to. This guy didn't exactly sound dangerous. If you ask me, I thought he sounded scared."

McManaway laughed. "You mean you've been doing this so long, Harter, that you can tell if someone *sounds* dangerous?"

"Mind games," Harter answered. "So'd you do your shopping today? Did you buy what you need for the baby's room?"

"Yeah."

"Is it going to be a boy or a girl?"

"Don't know."

"I thought all the upwardly mobile parents these days had it all checked out, so they know what to expect."

"I told Sally I didn't want to know."

"I wouldn't either," said Harter as he reached for the door handle. "Chance keeps it interesting, doesn't it?"

A minute later, walking across the parking lot, he did have to admit he was taking a chance. You always had to wonder if you were being set up. Still, he'd picked the meeting place, and the guy had begun by mentioning the bones. Like chance, there was something to be said for nervousness. It kept you ready. He *had* done dumber things.

Once he was on the station platform, the solitary rap of his soles seemed to ripple up the concrete ahead of him until the echo was lost somewhere in the darkness. He glanced down at his watch and decided to kill the ten minutes left by sitting on the station porch. From the bench near the door, he had a clear view of the whole platform.

When he was young, when railroading was still trying to kick, that platform had never been completely empty, no matter what the hour. Now there were only two passenger trains a day—morning and evening Amtraks—and the riders went directly to the parking lot, never setting foot inside the station. No porters rushed about pushing full baggage carts, no crowds of excited relatives waited, no steam hissed out around big iron wheels. There was little evidence that this had once been the proud center of a proud city.

He turned to study the underpass. His caller, whoever it had been, might emerge from it at any moment. Desiring secrecy, as the guy apparently did, he might decide to park at the hotel lot across the tracks so he could come and go without Harter writing down his license plate number. Or maybe he didn't have a car. Maybe he was on foot.

Just after eleven, Harter stepped down from the porch and walked slowly toward the underpass, half-expecting the guy would come up out of the ground like the molemen. They'd become embedded in his head from a movie—*Superman and the Molemen*, or *Superman Meets the Molemen*, or some title he couldn't recall. They came up from the ground in the nighttime city, out of steaming manhole covers, out of scrap-metal heaps, out of smoky pits at the dump. Only Clark Kent in his Superman guise could foil their evil designs.

Going home the night they'd seen the movie, he and Terry, his best friend in elementary school, had sidestepped every manhole cover, stayed away from every sewer grate, so as not to anger the sinister spirits. A freight had blocked the crossing and, with a curfew to beat, they'd been forced to use the underpass, the dreaded foot tunnel from downtown, under the five tracks, into their own East End.

The tunnel was always wet with groundwater and always smelled like piss, or maybe it was beer, and the winos squatted against the damp underground walls.

He and Terry were barely down into it when the dimness scared them and the dampness chilled them, and without a word passing between them, they each imagined the subterranean molemen and started running like hell, leaping over a drunk's legs so as not to be tripped, finally running up the steps, two at a time, running until they were halfway up the hill to their homes. Until they were in safe terrain. Where the molemen couldn't get them.

Anything could happen, and the nervousness kept you ready.

He thought he heard something and stopped fast.

His hand slid inside his jacket and gripped his gun.

Slowly, he turned around, checking the station platform from different angles.

He could have sworn he'd heard—or sensed—something, but there was only the empty platform.

He looked at his watch again. *Twelve minutes after eleven.*

He lit a cigarette, then headed toward the underpass, and when he reached its mouth, he hesitated only a second before he started down the steps, unsure whether he was still searching for his caller or confronting the old fear.

The underground walkway wasn't used much anymore since the crossing was rarely tied up for long, but every few years citizens demanded that the city council and railroad authorities throw the winos out and fix the damn thing up. These days the underpass was in one of its cleaner, well-lit incarnations, though it still smelled faintly of urine and spilled booze. Cigarette butts and slivers of glass littered the shattered concrete floor, but there was nothing more to be seen.

It was nearing midnight when Harter climbed back in the car.

"Well," said McManaway, "I didn't hear any shots. What'd your man have to say?"

"No one showed," said Harter. "No one showed."

... 14 ...

"I shot her."

Christ, here he was again. Darrell Phillips. Sunday morning, and for the second time in four days the appliance dealer was spouting the same confession.

Harter stared across the interrogation table and watched Phillips rub at the Styrofoam cup. "You say you shot your wife. Why?"

Somehow he didn't expect a coherent response, and he didn't get one. Phillips looked up, his weak mouth opened, and out came "Because." Then he stopped. *Because.*

The guy's head dropped, his dazed eyes lowered toward the scratched table, his puffy fingers stroked the cup, and he seemed to dive into himself. Harter wished he could come up with something reasonable to ask, but he knew there was little use. He'd just wait for the report from the apartment. This time he hadn't bothered to send anyone but Dave McManaway to the store near the viaduct. He had a pretty good notion what McManaway's report would be.

Phillips' face wasn't such an emotionless pancake makeup mask this morning, or maybe Harter was just fooling himself by believing he could spot the pain in it.

He decided to try again. "Your wife says you were in Vietnam."

"My wife is dead. I shot her," said Phillips.

"I know other Vietnam vets are troubled by what happened there," said Harter, staying on the course he'd selected. "Could be you need to talk to somebody about it. The war's been over for ten years. You've got to get it out of your mind some time. We all do things we'd just as soon forget. Being a cop, I've had to shoot criminals. I've killed a few. You can only tell yourself that you were doing the right thing at the time, that you had no other choice. You were in a war, whether you wanted to be there or not."

Harter imagined he sensed Phillips clench his teeth, but that was the extent of it. The little sermon obviously wasn't leading anywhere fruitful. The storekeeper just seemed to retreat more. Perhaps, somewhere inside, he was caught up in his own mind games, worried about the emerging molemen with no Superman to fight them for him, facing his own flooded warehouses, haunted places, pedestrian underpasses. A hell of a week it had been.

Harter pushed forth a pawn. "When were you in Vietnam? The late sixties?"

The silence was becoming irritating by the time McManaway opened the interrogation room door and waved Harter out to the hall. There again stood Mrs. Phillips, alive and breathing, and looking like she'd taken more time getting dressed than she had three mornings before. Maybe she'd been getting ready for church when McManaway had arrived.

"Your husband has the same story he did on Thursday," Harter told her.

Rather than blow out the confidence she had the first time, Vi Phillips seemed genuinely confused. "I don't know what to do, Detective. I don't know what Darrell went through in the war. I don't know anything about those times, or his childhood, for that matter, except what he's told me. I'm not from Shawnee originally. I just don't know what to do."

"You promised to take him to a doctor."

"He has an appointment tomorrow." She reached up and twisted a red curl. "I told you, he's just been under so much pressure. I don't know what else it could be. I don't know if it's memories of Vietnam, or the flood, or what. Sometimes it's like he's off in the wild blue yonder."

"I'd judge that's where he is right now, Mrs. Phillips. Off in the wild blue yonder. Did anything go wrong last night?"

She shook her head. "Everything was perfectly normal. When I went to bed, he was watching the late movie. I don't even know what it was."

"You didn't argue? He wasn't drinking?"

"I told you—Darrell's not a drinker," she said, her testiness surfacing. "He doesn't take drugs, either, if that's your next question." The red curl was now so twisted out of shape that it curved like a spike away from the rest of her hair. "Darrell didn't actually do anything illegal, did he? He didn't kill me or anyone else."

"He can't just keep walking in here and confessing to murder."

"What are you suggesting?"

"I'd like to take him over to Shawnee Mental Health Center. They have a weekend distress center. Weekends and holidays are often their busy times. Somebody there could talk to him and keep an eye on him, and you could take him to your own doctor tomorrow like you planned. We could call ahead, and you could sign him in and out. There'd be no court orders or anything."

"Darrell hates shrinks."

"I'm not so fond of them myself, but this can't go on. It's not doing anyone any good."

"What if they decide to keep him? What if they send him to the state mental hospital at Crimpton? It's a horrible place. You wouldn't do that to a responsible citizen, a businessman, would you? You might as well put him in jail."

Harter had to agree: Crimpton State Mental Hospital was a terrible place. Once he'd taken a tour of it with a police group, and for a week afterward he kept picturing the overcrowded wards where men and women shuffled along hallways, passed their time in front of TV sets, simply waited to see which one would wail out first. If you weren't crazy when you went in, you just might be when you got out.

"I don't believe they'll send your husband to Crimpton, Mrs. Phillips. They don't do that much anymore, especially if you're going to get private treatment for him. I'm trying to find a way to let you avoid trouble."

Vi Phillips seemed to be weighing her choices. Finally she said, "Okay."

Harter tried not to show his relief that she'd caved in. His bluff had worked. He had no idea what he'd have done if she'd refused to take her husband for observation. And, whatever Darrell Phillips' problems, Crimpton *was* too large a specter to want to face.

A few minutes later, he stood in the parking lot and watched Mrs. Phillips drive away with her husband in the back seat and Dave McManaway next to her in the front. Harter had convinced her she oughtn't make the transport alone, just in case something went wrong, and she'd convinced him Phillips would be more relaxed and comfortable in their own car. McManaway riding shotgun was the compromise.

He killed a little time outside, smoking a cigarette and staring at the mountains, and then he went in and chatted for a while about Saturday night's calls with Herr, the desk cop. When he'd heard enough, he impounded the Sunday paper and slipped away to his office.

A photo of the Governor and Senator, smiling with over-size scissors in their hands, was on the front page of *The News*. Inside, a full page of the local section was consumed by scenes of the museum opening. The politicians would be in heaven this morning. He wasn't, however.

He came across a story about the state's appeal to designate the flooded region as a federal disaster area, but three sentences into it, his mind drifted and he gave up trying to concentrate. He wandered down the hall to find a cup of coffee, and when McManaway returned, he was sitting in his chair, holding the Styrofoam cup, reading the numbers on the calendar on the wall, wondering if he should go visit Liz that afternoon, or whether he should keep working and go see Flathead Nash a day early. Nash would probably be home. It was Sunday, and the bars wouldn't be open for a few more hours.

"Well, I guess that's taken care of," said McManaway as he dropped into Caruthers' seat. "Hell, Mrs. Phillips didn't even make me hike back here. She gave me a ride. You gave her a pretty rough time."

"Not as rough as if her husband had *really* killed her," Harter answered. "I don't want to be responsible for him, do you? She's not really thinking of what's best for him, anyway. She's just concerned about their reputation, their standing in the community. Christ, she'll have him signed out before breakfast tomorrow."

"Have you ever had a case where a Vietnam vet went off the deep end?"

"Not really. I don't think it's as common as TV would have you believe. Oh, I've arrested a couple guys who claimed they got screwed up in Vietnam, but I also know a guy who claims he

91

got screwed up in World War Two and has never been the same."

"I probably should know more about Vietnam than I do," said McManaway. "I seem to have missed most of it. I was still in high school when the war ended. I hear people talk about the Sixties, but I can't say I understand all the tensions there must have been."

"I don't know that anyone does."

"What do you think will become of Phillips?"

"Got me. How about this, though? Someday when you've caught up on the phone calls about the bones, after you've finished sorting through the files and all, suppose you try and check out Phillips' military record. With any luck, we won't see him again, but if we do, it might be useful to know more about him."

McManaway nodded agreement. "Sounds reasonable," he said, but Harter had already turned away and was flipping through Caruthers' report of the 1967 hit-and-run.

When the ring destroyed the silence, the two of them stared at each other for a moment before McManaway reached for the receiver. Almost immediately, Harter wished he'd been the one to pick up the phone. The young cop's expression had turned so serious that he wondered if Sally had gone into labor early, if something awful had happened.

Finally, McManaway hung up and looked over at him. "They've found a body."

"Yeah?"

"They think it's Roger Wilton."

··· 15 ···

Harter and McManaway were barely out of their car before Wayne Smith was crossing the parking lot toward them. Actually, he was Sergeant Wayne Smith, and he headed the state police detachment in the county.

They were standing in a graveled pulloff with three picnic tables, high on the old Ohio Road atop Black's Mountain. All around them, state troopers wandered about, searching the road, the bushes, the autumn-thinned woods for anything out of the ordinary.

"Where's the body, Wayne?" Harter asked.

Sergeant Smith nodded over at a picnic table near the trees. Harter could see the gray hair of someone leaning over something on the other side of the table. He recognized Pete Epstein.

"It's out of your jurisdiction, of course, but we contacted you anyway," said Smith. "I remembered McManaway asking us about Roger Wilton and a bunch of others on Friday. I figured you'd want to be in on this."

"You know why we're interested, I guess—all about the bones in Shantytown?" asked Harter.

"Half the world must have heard that story by now."

"Seems like it."

"Are you sure it's Roger Wilton?" asked McManaway.

Smith looked a little taken aback by the rookie detective's question. "It's either your Roger Wilton, or someone planned this all out and went to a hell of a lot of trouble with falsified license photos and everything." He pulled a wallet out of his pocket and handed it over to Harter. "We found this on the ground at the edge of the woods. There's no money in it, but I don't see this as a robbery. Someone stole whatever cash there was and tossed the billfold into the brush. I'd say it was an afterthought. We found a checkbook, too, and it was still in Wilton's back pocket."

The driver's license was from North Carolina and showed a Charlotte address. ROGER NASH WILTON. His mother had given him her maiden name as a middle one. BORN 7/27/48. MALE. WHITE. 160 LBS. 5'11". BROWN EYES.

Harter flipped through the plastic and found a Social Security card and a telephone calling card, but no credit cards. The only personal photo was an old, creased black-and-white of a grade school boy with unruly dark hair and fine features, just as Matt Curry had described the young Roger Wilton. The boy was next to a porch swing, and sitting on the swing was a woman in her thirties. From her hairdo and clothes, Harter judged the picture had been snapped one afternoon in the early or mid-1950s. He had no doubt that he was seeing Roger and Nan Wilton on the porch of the Egypt Street house.

Odd. Dorothy Merrill had claimed she didn't know where to lay her hands on a photograph of her mother, but her brother had carried one around with him all these years.

"The checkbook has the same North Carolina address as the driver's license," said Sergeant Smith. "No wife's name's on the checks. The entry book shows that two days ago Wilton wrote a check for two hundred and ninety dollars, which just about cleared the account. We can't find any sign of a car, but it's obvious he didn't jog up here from Charlotte. No sign of keys either. I guess when we find the car, we find the keys."

"Huh," mumbled Harter, not really concentrating on what Smith was saying. Instead, he was trying to force entry into the scene of the small boy and his mother, as if it were possible to climb up the porch steps, be there with them on the swing, and overhear their conversation.

Curry had described Nan as a good-looking woman, and he'd been right. It was easy to feel her appeal, even in the worn snapshot. Nothing about her relaxed pose, however, hinted at her alleged wild temper. She didn't look like the sort to batter heads with skillets or throw knives in uncontrollable rage, but then, you never could tell. She didn't emit an aura of craziness at all, not even the toughness that so many middle-aged South Shawnee women did. There was something vulnerable about her. And from the way she eyed her son, Harter could imagine the see-no-evil-in-Roger streak that Curry had also described.

"Can I keep this picture?" he asked.

"We'll have to follow evidence procedures," Smith answered.

"Damn, Wayne. I've been working on this case."

"Come on, Harter. What do you want me to do? We must be five miles outside the city limits. This isn't your terrain. I just can't hand everything over to you. Why do you figure Wilton was out here anyway?"

Harter shrugged. "Maybe he went for a drive with whoever killed him. Or maybe someone murdered him, then brought the body out to dump. Ever since they cut the interstate through the mountain to the north, there can't have been much traffic here. You know as well as I do that this thing started in Shawnee, no matter where the body was found."

"You sound like Pete Epstein." Smith pointed across the lot to where the medical examiner was still hunched over the body. "He thinks Wilton was dead when he was brought out here, too. If that's so, then the killer knew the area well. When he was looking for a dumping ground, he remembered this old picnic area."

"He probably used to park out here," said McManaway.

Harter handed the wallet back to Smith and moved fast toward Epstein. The chill November wind that sunny morning made him zip up his black jacket as he walked. Wayne Smith, with all his damn procedures, reminded him of Caruthers. Stick to the regulations, the book, the letter of the law. Forget the spirit. Forget you were trying to find a murderer. Harter hoped he'd have better luck with Pete Epstein, who was not so bound by jurisdictional lines. Epstein was medical examiner for the county as well as for the city.

Roger Wilton's corpse was flat on its back, about a yard on the other side of the picnic table. "How many bodies are we going to find this week, Pete?" asked Harter.

"At least I don't have to shovel around in the mud for this one," said Epstein, barely looking up.

"What do you think? No doubt it's Wilton?"

"Hell, the face matches the license photo, brown mustache and all. He appears to have been shot twice in the chest at a fairly close range. There's not much blood around, so I'd say the job was done somewhere else. When you find your killer, you might find traces of blood in his vehicle. The vehicle was parked over there. You can see the marks in the gravel from dragging the body by the feet from there to here. There aren't any clear footprints or tire tracks. The top of the mountain here

96

has dried out pretty much since the rains on Monday and Tuesday."

"When do you think he was shot?"

"Last night. Right now, I'd say before midnight."

"Sounds likely," said Harter.

"Why?" snapped Sergeant Smith. "You suddenly psychic, or what?"

"It's a lot simpler than that. A guy called me yesterday afternoon. He wouldn't tell me who he was, but wanted to know if I was the one investigating the bones at the Wilton place, and he wanted to meet me at eleven o'clock last night. I was there, but he wasn't. I'd bet the world it was Roger Wilton and the reason he didn't keep our appointment was that he'd gone to see someone else beforehand."

"And *that* someone else killed him?" asked McManaway.

"You got it."

"Two and two are usually four," said Pete Epstein as he rose out of his squat.

"I trust you'll see I get a copy of any report you give the state police," Harter said to him.

"It's public record. But don't expect much more than I've told you. We'll come up with a more exact time of death and some info about the weapon, but it'll most likely be pretty cut and dried."

"Thanks, Pete," said Harter, but he was actually glaring at Wayne Smith.

"You still want the goddamn photograph?" Smith asked.

"Sure. But I'll go through procedures. I wouldn't want to rock the boat. You know me, Wayne. Yes sir, no sir, every screw turned according to the manual."

Smith pulled out the wallet, opened the thing up, and slid the old picture free of its plastic casing. "Here, Harter. Shit.

97

Make yourself a copy and send me back the original. I don't even know what value it has."

"Neither do I," said Harter as he reached for the photo of Roger and his mother. "I just wanted it, Wayne. Maybe I'm sentimental."

"You son of a bitch."

Harter smiled. "I guess you guys are going to work the North Carolina end, aren't you? I mean, you'll contact people down there, for whatever good it is?"

"Yeah," said Smith.

"You'll keep us up to date?"

Almost begrudgingly, Smith nodded.

"Why don't you release the driver's license photo to the press?" asked Harter. "Wilton's vehicle has got to be parked someplace. Someone must have seen him in the last couple days. A picture in the newspaper could cut out a lot of legwork."

"Any other orders, General?"

"Prepare to attack at dawn." Harter turned to McManaway. "You ready to go?"

They were halfway down Black's Mountain when McManaway piped up. "You were pretty rough on him."

"On Wayne Smith? Hell, he's been rough on me before. It all evens out. Is *rough* the word for the day? You said I was rough on Vi Phillips, too."

"So what do you want to do now?" McManaway asked.

Before answering, Harter stared out the windshield at the road screwing down. What he wanted to do, how he wanted to spend the rest of the day, where he wanted to be, wasn't necessarily what he'd end up doing. He had a hunch he might end up driving through the West Side past Liz's studio, or out on the overlook studying the Sunday-calm city, but first . . .

"First, we're going to drop you off at your place so you can have Sunday chicken with Sally," Harter told McManaway. "The two of you aren't going to see many more quiet afternoons. Soon there'll be a crying, hungry, wet baby around. Once I unload you, I'll be heading out the Avenue to let Roger Wilton's father and sister know what happened. They shouldn't have to hear it from an absolute stranger or read it in the paper."

"What I meant," said McManaway, "was what do we do next to find the guy who killed Wilton?"

Harter dodged the ball. "Why are you so sure it's a guy?"

... 16 ...

The silence roared so loud it nearly gave him an earache. As he watched the old man stare out his bedroom window, Harter kept seeing the vacant eyes of Darrell Phillips, the man who imagined he'd murdered his wife. Crazy, how a mind works overtime to fabricate connections, intertwinings between people, events, places that have nothing to do with each other on the surface, except they've crossed your life somehow, or your life has crossed them.

Wheat Wilton simply sat in his chair, his eyes hypnotized by the brick wall across the Avenue. If anything was happening inside his stricken brain, there was no way to find out. At least Harter couldn't come up with a way. Damn, he wished he could stick a needle into Wilton's thin arm and draw out facts and memories like a Red Cross nurse draws out blood.

Standing in the doorway of the bedroom, Harter felt like a cruel inquisitor. Dorothy Merrill had argued that her brother had been out of her father's thoughts for more than seventeen years and it could only harm the old man to tell him about Roger. Still, Harter couldn't shake off Thursday afternoon, when he'd mentioned Matt Curry and sensed some response in Wheat Wilton's eyes. He believed the boy's name might jar something loose, too. Eventually Dorothy had given in and had slowly led him up the steps. Now, faced with the old man, Harter began to think he was making a mistake, and a harsh one at that.

At least Dorothy was taking her good slow time working up to it. She was small-talking with her father in a tone that was gentler and more soothing than her everyday voice, and now and then, she glanced at Harter to be certain he hadn't changed his mind.

Neither Dorothy nor Bill Merrill had shown much emotion when Harter broke the bad news to them. Bill had reached for the remote control and turned down the television volume, then slumped back in his chair. Dorothy had turned a bit white, then seated herself on the end of the couch near her husband. After a minute the color had returned to her face and she'd said, "So that's how it ends."

So that's how it ends. So that's what became of Roger. It wasn't like she was particularly surprised. It was like she'd just finished watching a movie. *So that's how it ends.*

Now she was getting to the point with her father. "You remember Detective Harter, Daddy? He came to visit the other day." The old man stared. "Well, he's come back. He says Roger has returned to Shawnee."

She stopped, and both she and Harter studied Wheat Wilson's face for some flicker.

Nothing.

Nothing at all.

Dorothy's lips were beginning to form words. She was about to inform her father that Roger had been found dead. But before she launched into it, she looked again at Harter. It was too cruel a move, he decided. He shook his head to tell her to freeze those words before they came out.

"No?" she whispered.

He shook his head again and walked out into the hall.

He heard her say, "I'll bring you your Sunday dinner in an hour or so, Daddy," and then she too left the room and joined him at the top of the stairs. "I'm glad you backed off."

"Hell, it wasn't going to do any good anyway."

"I told you that before we came upstairs."

"I didn't want to hurt him, didn't want to make him worse."

Halfway down the steps, she turned and said, "You have a heart after all, huh?"

Yeah, he had a heart. Dorothy Merrill, like Vi Phillips and probably a lot of others, might doubt it, but he surely had a heart, and sometimes it hurt, though he wasn't fond of letting anyone know. Not even Liz.

Downstairs, he sat at the kitchen table, trying to figure out what to ask next, trying to get himself back on track, while Dorothy puttered around opening the oven and inspecting the ham that was baking.

"It was probably a lousy idea to come here this afternoon," he said. "But it made sense at the time. I thought I might as well tell you about your brother myself. I bet the state police will contact you before long. They might even want you to identify the body."

"God, what an awful idea." She opened a cabinet, took down two cups, poured coffee into them, and brought one over to him. "Did you say Roger was living in North Carolina?"

"According to his driver's license."

"Was he married? Did he have any kids?"

"We don't know yet."

"I can't believe that unreliable bastard would ever settle down and support a family," said Bill Merrill.

Harter felt like he'd lost the edge. He hadn't even noticed Dorothy's husband had entered the kitchen and was leaning against the wall behind him. Luckily, Bill Merrill wasn't a big bruiser with a switchblade in his hand, hiding in a dark underpass. Well, hell, he *was* a big bruiser, but at least he wasn't carrying a knife, and he hadn't exactly jumped out of the shadows like one of the molemen.

"You don't speak very highly of your late brother-in-law," Harter said to him.

"I've had to work for everything I ever got. Roger had it all handed to him, and he wasted it away. Not that Dorothy's people had much, you understand, but whatever the boy wanted, her mother saw that he got it. All the time I was working in the steel mill and sweating to make mortage payments on this place and raising sons, Roger was loafing at college and being handed his heart's desire. And I mean loafing. He decked out like a hippie and talked against the war and all. He was into drugs, too, if you ask me."

"You don't know that for sure," said Dorothy, cutting him off. "We never saw much of Roger. By the time he was out of high school, Bill and I had been married for years. Besides, we don't know what he did after he left home. He could have straightened up."

"I know what Wheat said about him," said her husband.

Harter wished he could disappear so he wouldn't intimidate the Merrills from really going at each other about Dorothy's brother. But they were aware of his presence, and despite the hard stares they threw at each other, they fell into a silence as thunderous as the one that swirled around Wheat Wilton's head upstairs.

Odd, for Dorothy to be so suddenly protective of her younger brother. Only three days before, she'd made no pretense about the fact she had no use for Roger. Harter wondereed if it was always like that, if people always defended their own kin, even when they felt otherwise, if the Merrills had been fighting this same argument for twenty years, or if Roger's death had merely opened some soft vein of family reveries in her.

She wasn't wearing her Shawnee Bombers T-shirt today, but rather a burgundy dress, as if she'd just come back from church. Even dressed up, she reminded Harter of his first impression of her. There was something about her face that just missed being pretty. She'd probably never been really pretty. She didn't much resemble her mother, the striking woman in the old photo in his pocket. On impulse, to wreck the heavy quiet and start them talking again, he pulled out the picture. "This was in Roger's wallet."

Merrill grabbed it before his wife could move. "That's Roger and Nan." He walked across the linoleum and surrendered the photograph to Dorothy. "When would you say— 1955 or so?" As she stared at it, he got himself a cup and poured some coffee. Then he leaned his big frame against the stove next to his wife.

For a moment, Harter thought she was going to cry. But, just as she'd recuperated fast from the news of her brother's death, Dorothy Merrill recovered again. She returned the snapshot to Harter and sank into a chair at the table. "I can almost remember the day Daddy dug out his old box camera and took that picture."

"Mother and son," mumbled Harter. Then, speaking clearer: "He does look like the apple of her eye. Actually, Matt Curry said exactly what your husband did—that your mother spoiled your brother a lot."

"Matt Curry, again," she said, a little sarcastically. "But I guess they're right. She sure went out of her way to cater to Roger."

"Bent over backwards," added Bill Merrill. "You'd have thought he was her only child. I don't believe Dorothy ever felt like her mother really loved her."

Another cold stare passed between the Merrills, almost like she was angry he had divulged another confidence. This was obviously not a day Dorothy Merrill would choose to live again.

"I've met Nan's brother," said Harter, trying to steer them to a new subject. He omitted mentioning that Matthew Curry had been with David Nash at the museum opening. "What do they call him—Flathead? I'm supposed to talk to him more tomorrow. Does he keep in touch with you?"

"He came to see Daddy on Friday. I don't know the last time we saw my uncle. It was probably all the stories about the bones that made him come. He was always pretty close to my mother, but not particularly to the rest of us. He'd do things to make her happy. When he'd come by, he'd always have candy in his pocket, especially for Roger, but he never really stayed long. He'd make other stops on Egypt Street, like—"

"Like?"

"Like Matt Curry," she finished. Then she tried to cover up the awkwardness by asking, "Do you know anything new about the bones?"

"We feel they date to the mid-sixties, and that they're the remains of a young woman. I figure Roger would have been in high school or college at the time."

"Then you think they have something to do with him?" asked Bill Merrill.

Harter shrugged. "The news apparently brought him back."

"Nothing he could have done would surprise me, not that one," said Merrill.

"I keep wondering whether whatever happened is also connected with Nan Wilton being killed in the hit-and-run, or whether it's just coincidence," said Harter.

"God," said Dorothy. "It's awful to have all this stuff dragged back up. The last couple days, people seem to be looking at us different, like we had something to do with the body. I keep telling everyone I left Egypt Street long ago. Then they ask about Daddy. He'd have been there. When word gets out about Roger, people will really ask questions."

Harter thought she seemed more upset over what people might think than she had over hearing about her brother's murder. But maybe that wasn't so strange a reaction, he decided.

"What time is it?" asked Bill Merrill, as if to break up the conversation.

"Almost two," answered Dorothy. "We'll have to get a move on if we're going to have dinner before you go to work."

Harter recognized an exit cue when he heard one. "Where do you work now that the steel mill's closed?" he asked Merrill.

"I've got two jobs actually. Neither's much better than minimum wage. I work weekdays as a custodian and part time, like this evening, at a convenience store over on Furnace Street. Hell, I can see the mill from there. No matter what they say, it's still tough times. They may be creating a bunch of jobs, but none of them pay what the old ones did. Try and hold a family together and pay doctors' bills and all, and you'd see. Dorothy works, too. She's a waitress two nights a week. She'd work more if she could, but someone has to take care of Wheat. If he didn't get his railroad retirement, I don't know what we'd do."

"Did you work last night?" asked Harter as he stood up. He knew the question was transparent, that it was obvious he was trying to find out what they might have been doing when Roger was killed.

"I didn't," said Merrill. "Dorothy did, until about ten-thirty. I was here with Wheat. We told you, we didn't see Roger. We had no idea he was back in town."

Harter started for the back door and, just before going out, turned and said, "Good luck." He was nearly to the gate at the

106

end of the alleyway when he realized he was still holding the photo of Nan and Roger. He stuffed the picture in his pocket, pushed open the gate, and stepped into the Avenue. As he opened his car door, he glanced up at the second-floor window of the Merrill house. Inside sat Wheat Wilton, like a goddamned sphinx.

··· 17 ···

He was up at the overlook on the mountain, leaning against his car, surveying his domain, Shawnee, when he noticed that, down in the bottom of the bowl, the river was slowly rising, like God was ladling more milky soup into it and Mother Nature, Earth Goddess, was smiling her approval.

The thick river water was starting to wash out of its trench and over the towpath along the canal. As it slithered across the floodplain, it began to swirl, churning up topsoil, all the while making its way toward Egypt Street. It was like he had binocular vision, he could see it so clearly, so closely.

Outlined in a second-story window was an old man, and Harter had no trouble focusing in on the solemn face of Wheat Wilton staring out at the river pouring across the field toward his house. He could zero right in on the old man's eyes, and as if he could read Wheat Wilton's mind, he sensed the old man knew tragedy was coming. But down on the front porch— somehow Harter could see straight through the house with an X-ray vision like Superman's—on the front porch an attractive woman sat on a swing watching a boy, and the two of them were unaware—at least he believed they were unaware—of the impending flood, years ahead of them.

Across the street, another man sat on a porch, and even though the fellow looked only about forty, Harter knew the solid, muscled guy was Matt Curry. Matt Curry, just staring across Egypt Street. Whether he was monitoring the river sprinting toward him or whether he was studying Nan and Roger Wilton, Harter couldn't tell.

The water rose another notch, edging closer to the shed behind the Wilton's home, and Curry's face seemed to age a year with every foot the foul, muddy river gained on the shed. First the smile creases near his thin lips became deeper, spaded in, and then the lips themselves seemed to drop a bit—in sadness?—and the eyes lost a few degrees of their sparkle, and the forehead sprang a wrinkle and elongated as the hairline receded, and the hair turned from dark to gray, strand by strand, line by line, sparkle by sparkle.

A car, a 1950s Plymouth, long and low, with sharp pointed wings, sped along the street, screeching to a halt between Nan Wilton and Matt Curry. A red-faced man with a flattop stuck his head out the Plymouth window and waved and then, as if he caught sight of the high water coming, tore away in a fog of exhaust.

By now the boy, Roger, was a teenager. He scurried off the porch and peeked around the side of the house, looking back at the shed, like he was suddenly aware it was in danger, like he was suddenly aware of danger. He turned, called something to his mother, and as his lips moved he grew older still, his body filling out to adult size, his dark hair lengthening to a Beatles cut, then growing on past it until it is as long as a San Francisco hippie's, and it must be 1967, Roger's last full year in Shantytown, the year his mother is killed, the year all hell breaks loose, like a river out of its banks, and there are antiwar demonstrations and Lyndon Johnson, drawling Texan, is president and Vietnam draft calls are high. In another part of

Shawnee, a young Darrell Phillips is nervously opening an invitation from Uncle Sam.

Now Roger Wilton has an earring in his hand, a half-moon of ivory, and in his mouth is a cigarette. His mother doesn't seem to notice. It is hand-rolled, a sloppy job, and he lights it and inhales deeply and it's like he lifts off the ground just as the shed is lifted out of the backyard and begins to float downstream to Paw Paw, Hancock, Shepherdstown, Harpers Ferry, and on to Washington, like stops being announced by a railroad conductor.

Everything is underwater now. All of Shantytown. Harter twists his neck so he can see upstream, upriver toward the downtown flood-control walls. He is young himself, standing with his father watching the high walls be put up, and now they are in place and the creek is rising, coming up under the West Side bridge, threatening to drift one-half of the city away from the other, separating his East End from Liz's West Side.

Through the downpour, he can see Liz standing on the West Side bank. He wants to cross over to her, but the high waters turn him back, and all he can do is stand there as the river widens between them. And now the molemen are coming. They canoe the dangerous river like they cannot be harmed. Anything can happen. They will beat him with their paddles if he tries to swim over. He knows they will beat him, but he wants to try anyway.

It's almost impossible to see Liz now. The rain is coming down so hard, the creek is risin', the ghost canoes, the floating bones, the soup keeps ladling down on top of him.

Metal spoon, lightning bolt.

Waterfall crash, thundershot.

In the midst of the torrent, a knockout bell.

Eyes forced open. Reach for the phone.

"You want me to come by and pick you up or you want to meet me at the motel?"

Still groggy. "What?"

"You mean you're not even up yet, Harter? It's Monday morning. This is Dave McManaway. The driver's license photo in the newspaper paid off. A guy called an hour ago. We know where Roger Wilton spent Friday night. We're checking for prints now. I left a message at headquarters for you, but I was starting to worry."

"Where are you?"

"The Goodnight Motel."

"On Gap Street?"

"You got it."

"I'll be there in twenty minutes."

He dropped the phone into its rack, gave his eyes a rub, then threw back the covers, swung his legs out of bed, and headed straight for the kitchen. He turned up the burner to reheat last night's coffee, still in the pot.

In the living room, he lit a cigarette and thumbed through the phone book for Flathead Nash's number. He'd have to postpone his visit with Nash for a few hours. He wondered whether Nash already knew about his nephew's death, or whether he'd be the one to break the news as he had with the Merrills.

Dialing, he glanced out the window, down toward the top floor and roof of the old passenger station, *the museum*. Off in the West Side distance, he could see the spire of the church near Pete Epstein's office. Looking a little south, he could almost see the roof of Liz's studio. It wasn't even raining.

··· 18 ···

The Goodnight Motel wouldn't have made any travel guide's list of five-star accommodations. The place might have seemed comfortable enough in the late 1940s when it was built, but somewhere down the years it had dropped into dinginess, and there was no way it could compete with the new Holiday Inn or any of a half-dozen other lodging establishments in the city. You almost expected the neon sign out front to blast CHEAP ROOMS on and off. Harter guessed that was why Roger Wilton had registered there. Roger had to make his couple hundred bucks last. Then again, Roger had been away for more than seventeen years, so the Goodnight could have been the only motel he remembered.

Even with its cheap rooms, Harter didn't believe the motel was going to benefit much from all those tourists Shawnee was supposed to attract in the future. It wasn't near the new railroad museum, or the park, or the big Victorian homes in the West Side, or any other spot that was likely to draw a crowd. The Goodnight was just inside the city line in South Shawnee, not far from the railroad yards and offices. Maybe that was another reason Roger had picked the place. It was close to Shantytown.

The customers in the motel's best days had probably been

people in town on railroad business. But later it had become little more than a string of rooms let for the evening. You could drive by almost any night, check out the license plates, and learn who was screwing who. Some of Shawnee's most illustrious citizens had rolled and tumbled on those lumpy mattresses. If you put cameras behind the mirrors on the walls, you could easily come up with the stuff of pornography or blackmail, but the camera lenses would have to be strong enough to shoot through the deposit of perspiration and semen on the cracked mirror glass.

McManaway was sitting on a plastic chair next to the bed, sorting through a tan travel bag, when Harter entered. "About time you got here. They took the fingerprints down to the lab a few minutes ago. I don't hold out much hope of them helping a lot. Could all belong to Roger Wilton. The motel owner says he didn't see anyone visit the room. Hell, with this place, the prints could belong to somebody who was here for an hour the night before Wilton showed up."

"When did Roger check in?" Harter asked.

"Friday night. He apparently went off a few times on Saturday. The owner says the last time he saw Wilton was about seven-thirty Saturday evening. He drove away and never came back. The guy's in his office if you want to talk to him."

"I'll get to him. What about the car? If Roger drove away Saturday night, where's his car?"

"We haven't found it, or the keys either. I've put out a bulletin on it."

"Good," said Harter, sitting on the edge of the unmade bed. "Did he register the vehicle with the motel?"

"Yeah. A 'seventy-nine Subaru with North Carolina tags."

Harter pointed to the tan plastic bag on the floor in front of McManaway. "Anything in there?"

"Clothes. An extra pair of jeans, a couple clean shirts, underwear, socks. I guess he figured he might be here a while. There's a toothbrush and a razor in the bathroom. Nothing unusual."

"No drugs?"

"We haven't found any."

"No diary or notebook or letters or list of phone numbers or something like that?"

McManaway shook his head.

Harter lit a cigarette and looked over at the mirror on the dirty wall. His eyes dropped to the scratched-up dresser below. "Drawers empty?"

"Yeah. Wilton didn't bother to unpack much."

On the stand beside the bed, next to a green glass ashtray, was a cassette tape recorder and a pile of cassettes. "Did he have good taste in music? Any John Lennon?"

McManaway smiled. "Some Beatles. It's mostly sixties stuff. That's probably all he listened to. I'm like that. We like the music we grew up with. I'll bet his car didn't have a tape player so he brought that along for the ride."

"Good bet," mumbled Harter as he reached toward the plastic cassette boxes. "Cream . . . Jefferson Airplane . . . the Grateful Dead . . . the Rolling Stones . . . Jimi Hendrix."

He reached over and pressed the play button to hear what Roger had been hearing shortly before his death. The machine immediately clicked off. Harter pushed EJECT and, when the door flipped up, removed the tape. It was a Maxell blank cassette, not a prerecorded one, and it was unmarked in any way. He slid the plastic container back into the recorder, punched REWIND, and watched the little reels turn until the left one was full and the right one empty. He rubbed his cigarette into the green glass, hit PLAY again, and turned up the volume.

At first there was only the static of blank tape. Then came the words.

What the fuck am I doing   Didn't want to do it then either

It was a male voice. Soft, not rough. Slightly southern, perhaps from years spent in North Carolina. Harter had no doubt he was listening to Roger Wilton. And he was sure it was the same person who'd wanted to meet him at the station.

Just talking into this damn box   Trying to get my thoughts ordered   Hard to line all the ducks in a row

The space between phrases heightened the uncertainty—the sadness—in Roger's voice. Harter could picture him lying on the motel bed late Friday night or Saturday afternoon, talking to himself, psychoanalyzing himself as the cassette recorder's built-in microphone picked up his words.

Didn't know what to do that night either   Nineteen sixty-seven   Mom   in the shed   Lucky the old man was away   They'd called him out to a train wreck in the country someplace and he was gone every night that week   We knew we had to do it then   The old bastard never would have understood   He'd have climbed on his high horse

The "old man" had to be Wheat Wilton. Matt Curry had told Harter that Roger's father had also been away the night Nan Wilton was killed. Whatever the old man would or wouldn't have understood in 1967 was a dead point. Wheat Wilton surely couldn't understand much now.

Mom said it wasn't good but it was right   She promised to help so   it didn't happen to me what—

A loud truck went by, blotting out the words. Harter pushed STOP, then REWIND to take the tape back a bit.

—tard never would have understood   He'd have climbed on his high horse   Mom said it wasn't good but it was right   She promised to help so   it didn't happen to me what—

There was the damn truck again. It was on the tape. Missing words, like a Richard Nixon Special. Truck passing.

—Night   In the shed   We pushed   We moved everything out of the way and kept dampening the ground so it was easier to dig   So the same

115

thing didn't happen to me   Christ, I can't do this   Can't risk putting this down on tape   Got people to see   Can't use their names   Have to change all the names like Dylan sang in "Desolation Row"   She—

There was a click and then, once more, only the hiss of blank tape.

After a while, Dave McManaway said, "He's probably erased the rest, if there was anything there to start with. What do you make of it?"

"I picture him lying in bed, all by himself, trying to make some sense of why he'd come back to Shawnee," said Harter. "Recording the words somehow helped him to think. Some people keep diaries, I suppose. Don't you ever talk to yourself like that?"

"Once in a while."

"So do I," said Harter, deciding Roger's monologue to a tape recorder wasn't a whole lot different than his trips to the overlook on the mountain south of town. Sometimes he had to change all the names too, throw them all in a pot, stir them up and see what brewed. "I'd say we now know a few things, though."

"Yeah?"

"Roger sure as hell knew who was buried in that shed, since he and his mother did the burying. His father was away, so I'd almost bet it was December Nineteen sixty-seven, maybe the same week Nan Wilton was killed in the hit-and-run. You suggested that yourself the other night at the train station. When you get back to headquarters, I want you to really comb Caruthers' report of the accident. I have to go see Nan's brother, then I'll be down. Take the tape and the recorder with you. Play the whole thing through just to be sure we're not missing something, that there's not something later on."

There was a rap at the door and Harter turned off the recorder before he motioned for McManaway to see who it was.

116

Who it was, was Sergeant Wayne Smith of the state police, and what he said was, "Thought I'd check this out myself, Harter. I shared our info with you. Now it's your turn."

"Look around all you like, Wayne. Nothing much here. The motel owner saw Roger Wilton's picture in the paper. I told you that might be worth a shot. You know, we can cuss the media all we like, but we're no better than politicians. We use them, too. Sometimes they make our job easier."

"What are you now, a political scientist?" asked Smith, but he was smiling.

"I'm a Renaissance man, didn't you know?"

"Is this the Renaissance?"

"Have you heard anything from North Carolina?"

"It's shaping up. Wilton lived in an apartment in Charlotte. Police down there didn't find much when they got in the place, but they've talked to a few people. Landlady says she saw Wilton get in his car Friday morning, which jibes with him showing up here that night. He didn't tell her where he was going, and she didn't notice if he was agitated or anything. Apparently, he changed jobs a lot. He's been working recently as a groundskeeper at a golf course."

"Any family?"

"Divorced. His ex-wife says they were married in Nineteen seventy-eight and separated two years later—right after their daughter was born. She believes Wilton just couldn't handle being a father. Everything was fine before the baby, but then he went crazy just going to work, coming home, and tending the kid. I guess some men are like that."

"*Some* men, maybe," said McManaway, expectant father.

"Did she say whether Roger ever talked about Shawnee?" asked Harter. "She have any notion why he would have returned here after the bones made the national headlines?"

"Not a clue. She knew he'd grown up in the mountains,

117

and that was about it. He told her he left Shawnee in the late sixties and hitchhiked across country a couple times in his hippie days, eventually landing in North Carolina. They never visited here and she never met any of his family. He led her to believe all his close relatives were dead."

"Maybe they were," said Harter, thinking of the photo of Roger and his mother.

"The ex-wife claims she hasn't seen much of him for years. Other than holidays, he didn't visit the daughter a whole lot. She had no idea he'd come up here. She doesn't even know if he had a girlfriend. We're trying to check on it."

"You know we haven't located his car yet?" said Harter. "A 1979 Subaru."

Smith nodded toward McManaway. "Your assistant here put out the call. My troopers are keeping their eyes open. I take it you'll see I get any reports on fingerprints and whatever you found here."

"Sure," said Harter, glancing over at the tape recorder. "How about Pete Epstein—has he sent you the autopsy yet?"

"Expect one this afternoon. You'll get a copy." Smith looked around the room. "If this place is a washout, I'd at least like to talk to the motel owner while I'm here."

The springs rattled as Harter pushed himself up from the bed. "I was just about to do that myself. Guy runs a nice place, doesn't he?"

"Wouldn't know. Never spent much time here," said Smith as they stepped out on the porch that fringed the row of boxes.

"Neither have I," said Harter. Then he said, "Wait a minute," and ducked back in the motel room. Whispering, so Smith couldn't hear, he told McManaway, "Make a couple copies of that tape and send one to Wayne."

··· 19 ···

The proprietor of the Goodnight Motel wasn't any more pleasant than the establishment he ran. He had a slight accent that Harter decided was British worn away from years in Shawnee. Every time the guy spoke, a spray of spit emerged with his words, making you want to stand on the far side of the drab office from him. What he had to offer wasn't worth the danger of being infected with his germs.

Roger Wilton had arrived after ten on Friday night, November 8. He'd paid in cash for three nights and suggested he might stay longer. He wasn't concerned with luxuries, just wanted the cheapest room available. He'd taken a few things out of his green Subaru and disappeared into number 14. The owner hadn't noticed any visitors, but he wasn't in the business of keeping track of such things. As far as calls, the rooms didn't have phones, so maybe Roger used the pay phone, he didn't know. Saturday morning, Roger had come into the office for a cup of coffee before driving off somewhere. By midafternoon he was back, and then he'd gone out again in the evening, about seven-thirty. The Subaru was still gone Sunday morning, but the motelkeeper didn't worry. He had his money up front. Besides, he never questioned people going about their business, and he never questioned their business. Wasn't until he saw the photo in the morning paper that he gave it much thought. He had no doubt the man in the picture—the man whose body had been discovered on Black's Mountain—had been his customer, so he'd phoned the cops. He hadn't touched anything in the room. He'd never laid eyes on Roger Wilton before Friday night, he insisted over and over, as if Harter and Smith were trying to blame him for something. He was only being helpful, playing the good citizen.

As Harter drove to Flathead Nash's, he hoped Nan's younger brother was also going to be helpful, would also play the good citizen. The little he'd seen of David Nash at the museum opening certainly hadn't been inspiring. When told that Harter wanted to ask him a few questions, his response had been, *Well, you can ask.* Any idiot could ask. Breaking through Nash's tough-guy act might be another matter.

Harter drove up the hill that divided South Shawnee and the East End. On the down side, he passed the elementary school where he had spent six years. Each morning, rain, snow, or shine, he'd hiked up the steep grade to school, but now, like so much of his childhood, it was gone. Or rather, it still stood there, like the passenger station, but it no longer served as a grade school. Now it was a senior citizens' center. You could spend both your first and your second childhoods there.

He turned onto the road that ran up to the hospital. Just past the huge building, he turned again and steered down a narrow street until he figured he was close to Nash's house. He parked in the first spot he came to, got out of the car, and began checking numbers.

Matt Curry had told him this was the neighborhood where Nan Wilton—*Nan Nash*—had grown up. Harter wondered what it would have been like fifty years before, and decided it would have been much the same. With one or two exceptions, the houses were older dwellings, two-story brick affairs crammed close together on the hilly, thin street. Most of the homes seemed well enough taken care of. Some of the tiny yards had the look of generations of tending.

Flathead Nash's place wasn't much different from the rest, though the windows could have used a washing and the white trimwork needed a painting.

When Harter had called Nash that morning to postpone their meeting, Nash had acted as if he didn't know his nephew's body had been found. He hadn't yet seen a newspaper and the Merrills hadn't bothered to let him know. There'd been a pronounced pause after Harter had dropped the knowledge on him. Harter had pondered whether he should call Matt Curry, too, but he wasn't sure why.

The Flathead Nash who opened the door, however, didn't appear any more morose or depressed than the Flathead Nash he'd run into at the station on Saturday. The big guy motioned him in without a word and led him through the front room and back to the kitchen. Nash wasn't the worst housekeeper that Harter had ever seen. A few newspapers littered the living room rug, and there was a bit of dust atop the coffee table, but the disarray wasn't out of control. Nash was wearing the same pants and shirt he had at the museum opening, and there was something almost swaggering, or staggering, about his gait as he padded through the house in his slippers.

Nash sat down at the kitchen table in the same place he'd obviously been vegetating before Harter had knocked. A beer, a pack of cigarettes, and an ashtray were laid out in front of him. Pushed off to one side was a plate that showed the remains of egg yellows.

Without an invitation, Harter sat across from him, near the back door. "This your family place? Is this where you and your sister grew up?"

"No, that's a few doors up the street," answered Nash in his rough voice. He lit an unfiltered Camel. "You want a beer?"

"I'll take some coffee if you got it," said Harter, lighting his own cigarette.

"Have to be instant."

"Fine with me."

Nash got up, went over to the stove, and turned on the burner under a teakettle that was next to an unwashed skillet with a spatula in it.

Harter watched him lift a cup off the drainboard, then find a clean spoon and a jar of instant coffee. "You still work for the railroad?"

"I don't work no more," said Nash without looking at him. "Bad back. I do a few odd jobs now and again. I make ends meet. The house is paid off."

"Everybody seems to have worked for the railroad, didn't they? You, Matt Curry, your brother-in-law Wheat."

"That's the way it goes, ain't it?"

There mustn't have been much water in the kettle because it was already whistling. Nash took a drag on his Camel, then poured hot water into the cup and brought the cup over to the table. He pointed toward a sugar bowl and a pint container of milk.

"Black," said Harter.

"Eat out your insides," said Nash, reaching for his beer.

"Sorry I surprised you with the news of your nephew."

"It was a surprise and it wasn't. Never figured I'd hear of him again, but I always did figure he'd end in a bad way."

"What do you mean?"

"I mean what I said. After he drifted off all those years ago, I knew we'd hear some day that he was dead. I'm sure plenty of people always figured I'd end in a bad way, too, but I'm still here, cussing and grouching."

"Roger didn't try to contact you Friday night or Saturday, did he?"

"Don't know whether he tried or not. He never got me if he did."

"What'd you think of your nephew?"

"I think he did what the hell he wanted, and I ain't going to jump on him for that. If you ask me, he should have gone in the Marines, but that's water over the dam. Nan spoiled him, but Roger and I always got along."

"I hear she'd go along with whatever he wanted."

"You heard right."

"But Wheat wouldn't."

"Don't see Wheat as no kind of hero. Nan was the one with a temper, but Wheat could be mean enough. He wasn't the sort whose blood boiled. He was one of them that calculated everything."

"Did he and Nan fight?"

"Don't know what went on when they was in private. Wasn't no business of mine."

"How'd they get together, the two of them?"

"I was little and didn't pay much attention. Nan was eight years older than me. She was working in the union office when she met him, and then she got pregnant, though my mother never wanted none of us to say so out loud. So they got hitched, that's all. Wasn't the way Ma wanted it."

"What do you mean?"

"Ma wanted Nan to be a nurse, 'cause she herself always wanted to be a real nurse. See, Ma was sort of a midwife. This was a long time ago, you know. Women didn't have all their babies in hospitals, particularly in South Shawnee and out in the country. They couldn't afford to in the thirties. So they'd call Ma and she'd help deliver 'em. I always judged that's why she wanted a house up here by the hospital. It made her feel official somehow, being up here near regular doctors and nurses. Anyway, she wanted Nan to be a real nurse. She was supposed to work in the union office a couple years, save her money, and then go to nursing school, but it all fell apart. She got knocked up and wound up with Wheat."

"Did your sister ever try to go back to school after she was married?"

"She had Dorothy, then Roger, and Wheat wouldn't hear of it. A man's supposed to support his family, he claimed. I know what he meant, but she could have been a good nurse. So could Ma have. Nan was a hell of a lot brighter than Wheat. She got all the brains in the family, not me. Roger was smart, too, but he didn't always show it."

"You're not very fond of your brother-in-law, are you?"

"Just because Wheat's old and sick don't mean he ain't an asshole."

"You remember an article from a year or two ago—about two brothers in Massachusetts who didn't speak for twenty-five years, then died on the same day?"

"Hell, you wishing a stroke on me? No matter what I thought of him, Wheat's goddamn sad enough now. I saw him the other day."

"The Merrills told me you went down there. Why?"

"The bones, I guess."

"You have any ideas about them?"

Flathead shook his head and reached for another cigarette.

"How about Roger? Any ideas about him?" asked Harter.

"Don't believe I seen him since Nan's funeral."

"Saturday, you told me you were out of town when she was run down."

"Yeah. I was back in time for the burying."

"Your brother-in-law was out of town the night it happened, too, wasn't he? Must have been a big shock to come home and find her dead."

"Must have. It was a shock for all of us."

"Roger was going to the community college at the time, right?"

"So they say. I couldn't prove it. Never been there."

"Was he upset at the funeral?"

"About as upset as anyone that's mother just got run over. What the hell kind of question is that?"

"Sorry. It was a bum thing to ask. But tell me, did you ever meet any of Roger's friends? Do you know if he had a girlfriend?"

"Wouldn't know no names or faces after all these years, if I ever did. The couple times I saw him, his hair kept getting longer and he was hanging around with others like that. No one paid me to keep tabs on him. Wasn't my job. I wasn't his old man."

"How did he get along with his sister and her husband?"

"Wouldn't know. Never stayed in touch with 'em."

"Dorothy seems to have been closer to her father than her mother."

Flathead gave a shrug, and Harter knew he'd just about pulled everything out of him that he was going to be able to. "Thanks."

"For what?" asked Nash.

"For the chat," said Harter, getting up from the table.

"No need to thank me. I ain't exactly inviting you to drop in whenever the hell you please."

"I ain't asking you to."

They were halfway through the front room to the door when Flathead stopped cold and pointed at a picture on the wall. "That's us, the whole clan. Ma, and my father, and me, and everyone on the day Nan graduated high school. I'm the little one, you believe that? Hair combed and everything. Times change."

Harter turned and stared at the hand-tinted photograph. Nan Nash, wearing a cap and gown, stood next to her proud mother. Clumped around them were the rest of the Nash family. It *was* hard to believe Flathead Nash had ever been a cheery-faced kid.

Nan appeared twelve or fifteen years younger than in the photo of her and Roger on the porch on Egypt Street, but he'd studied the other picture enough times to recognize her. If the colorist had it right, her long hair and clear eyes were both dark brown. Her bright red lips were curved into an enormous, unforced smile. She looked like she had the whole world ahead of her.

... 20 ...

He couldn't get Nan Wilton's face out of his head. Harter kept seeing her as he pulled away from the curb. But before he'd passed half a dozen houses, they called him on the police radio and her image immediately evaporated. They'd located Roger Wilton's car on the street in front of the high school, only a few blocks away. He turned onto the road that circled around by the hospital's emergency entrance and twisted its way uphill until it came out across from the school's football stadium. He knew the entwined streets as well as he knew the lines on his palm, and he knew where they seemed to break off or hit dead ends.

Wilton's green Subaru was parked almost straight across from the main doors of East Shawnee High, near three police cars. Uniformed cops surrounded the vehicle, checking it out every which way.

"No idea how long it's been there," a man was telling McManaway when Harter walked up. "No way to keep track of all the cars on this street. They had a football game Friday night, then some goings-on, a dance or something, Saturday night, and on weekdays the whole damn block is filled with students' and teachers' cars. You just can't worry about who's parked up here."

"What time on Saturday night was the dance over?" asked Harter, zeroing in on what seemed important.

"I don't know. Eleven, eleven-thirty. Before midnight, anyway," said the man. "Unless there's a ruckus, none of us pay much mind. It's the price you pay for living near a high school."

"Thanks," McManaway said to the guy. Then, as they walked toward the Subaru, he said to Harter, "At least the mystery of the missing keys is over. They were in the ignition. But I doubt Wilton drove the thing up here, unless he was pretty disconnected that night. The keys were inside and the doors were locked. I'd bet Wilton met his killer somewhere else, and that the car was parked here early Sunday morning, after the body was dumped on the mountain. The killer just locked the doors and walked away. Of course, it could be different. Maybe Wilton was meeting an old high school friend and this seemed like a good place to get together."

"Maybe," said Harter. "But I'd go with your first impulse. Let's say the car was dropped here later. So the murderer either lived close enough to walk home in the middle of the night, or had an accomplice, someone who picked him up."

"Or *her*," said McManaway, smiling.

"Or her." Harter drummed his fingers on the green metal of the car and stared through the windshield at the driver's seat. "They took prints, huh?"

"Yeah."

"I see we're the big show. Look over at the school."

Despite the fact that it was November, the classroom windows were wide open, and teenage bodies were leaning out of them, trying to get a better view of whatever the police were doing out front.

"Like a snowstorm," said McManaway.

"What?"

"Don't you remember being in elementary school and crowding around the windows all excited when it started to snow?"

Suddenly, Harter got the urge to go inside the building. If he was serious about tracking Roger Wilton's days in Shawnee, he'd probably end up there eventually, so it might as well be now, while he was already there. He'd wandered halfway across the street before he thought to call back to McManaway, "I'll be down at headquarters later."

"I left a copy of the tape and the autopsy on your desk," said McManaway, but by then Harter was climbing the bank of steps that led up to the stone plaza and the flagpole in front of East Shawnee High School.

One step inside the doors, and he was no longer sure where he was heading. Though he'd spent six years at East Shawnee, the school no longer belonged to him, and he felt like an alien. A sign inside the entrance reinforced the feeling: VISITORS MUST REPORT TO OFFICE. He hoped they hadn't moved the office. Two boys gave him long glances as he passed them in the locker-lined hall.

The desks may have been newer, and the long-legged secretary was sure prettier, but the office didn't look all that different from what he remembered. After he'd introduced himself, the secretary had gone down a corridor to one of the inner rooms, and before long a man in a gray suit was standing across the counter from him, holding out a hand to shake.

"Edward, isn't it? Edward . . ."

"Harter."

Mr. Adams, the principal, had always had a formal streak, had always refused to use nicknames. Adams had been Harter's eleventh-grade history teacher, and the students were all Edward, William, or Susan, never Ed, Mouthy, or Suzie. He'd had occasion to run into Adams over the years, or his former teacher probably wouldn't have been able to retrieve his name at all.

"What year was it you graduated?"

Harter got the impression that Mr. Adams opened many a conversation with the same question. "Nineteen sixty."

"My, my. I must have taught you my third year here. Seems so long ago, but I suppose it has been twenty-five years, hasn't it? I never had an inkling in those days that I'd become principal."

Nor had Harter. As he recalled it, discipline in the history teacher's class had been far less than shipshape. It was one of those rooms where the air was filled with spitballs and sometimes with textbooks. He'd always believed Adams had become principal by default. Either that, or he'd just piled up so many education courses and so much seniority that they couldn't deny him the job.

"You're with the police now, aren't you?" Adams always seemed to ask that question whenever Harter saw him, too.

"Yes."

"Well, what are they doing outside? Everyone wants to know. It's quite disrupted our day."

"It's a murder."

"A murder?" Adams sounded genuinely shocked, as if he was worried that one of his students had bumped someone off.

"You didn't happen to notice the story in the paper this morning about the body found on Black's Mountain, did you?"

"Why, yes, I did."

"The Subaru parked out front belonged to the victim, Roger Wilton. He graduated from here, too. We believe he might have been killed because of something that happened almost twenty years ago."

"Does it have something to do with those bones they found in South Shawnee? Isn't that what the article insinuated?"

"We're not sure, but since I was here, I thought I'd drop in and see if anyone can remember anything about Roger Wilton and who his friends might have been."

"Roger Wilton . . . The name sounds familiar. I might have even taught him. When would he have graduated, Edward?"

"Nineteen sixty-six, I think."

"I'll tell you, these days there aren't many of us here who might remember him. We've had more than our share of retirements and turnover in the past twenty years. Mr. Webster still teaches biology—I'm sure you recall him—and Mrs. Robbins is still the librarian, but they're about the only ones. It's all so long ago, you understand—Nineteen sixty, Nineteen sixty-six— they're like the distant past. Before all the turmoil. In those days, we didn't worry about students smoking marijuana in the lavatories, and we could send girls home when their skirts were too short. It was a different world, Edward. I preferred it myself."

"Where might I find Mr. Webster?" asked Harter, trying to avoid a nostalgia sermon.

"I believe he has classes until the end of the day. Why don't you go to the library and see Mrs. Robbins? She has a set of yearbooks up there. They could be of some help. I'll send a note to Mr. Webster's room and ask him to stop in and see you when school's over. There's only an hour left. Meanwhile, I'll try to get you a transcript of Roger Wilton's classes and grades, if you'd like. That's about all I can do."

"Fine," said Harter. "One more thing."

"Yes?"

"Was there a school dance Saturday night?"

"It was Homecoming."

Hell of a Homecoming for Roger Wilton, Harter thought. "What time was it over?"

"I'm positive everyone was out by eleven-thirty, unless the

band was still packing up their equipment. The cleanup committee came back yesterday afternoon to take down the decorations."

Harter nodded, started to leave the office, then turned back. "The library's where it used to be, isn't it?"

"Yes."

For a reason he didn't completely understand, he found himself taking the long way through the building. As he passed the gym, where flood victims had slept on cots for two nights the week before, a bell rang and kids swarmed out of the locker rooms. He was almost carried upstairs by the press of them, all the while feeling their eyes on him. He was glad when he found the library.

He recognized Mrs. Robbins, though he doubted he'd have known her if they'd met in the market. It hit him that she must have been pretty young in the late 1950s. He'd thought of her as older, but he guessed that was always true with kids and adults. Now she was probably in her early fifties, her hair was still blond, and she wore a trim, tailored red suit.

An English teacher was about to bring in her last-period class for a research project, she told him. But if he wanted to look through the old yearbooks, he was welcome, and she'd join him when she could. She motioned him to step behind the library counter and pointed out the yearbooks, all neatly arranged on two shelves. "The history of East Shawnee High," she informed him before moving off to greet the students filing in.

Just as he'd had the urge to enter the high school and take the roundabout route through the halls, Harter had an urge to look up his own graduating class, but he fought it off. Instead, he pulled 1965 and 1966 from a shelf and took the volumes into Mrs. Robbins' glass-walled office, as she'd directed. Before he sat down, he had another urge and returned to the shelves to collect 1940 and 1941. East Shawnee High, built in the Depression as a public works project, was only a few years old then, and he hadn't even been born, but he figured he'd find Nan Wilton there.

Sure enough, there was Nancy Nash, 1941, pearls around her neck, like the other girls. She hadn't been valedictorian or salutatorian or class president, but, despite the lack of glamorous titles, her peers had selected her "Most Likely to Succeed." There must have been something about her, some drive, some vibration, some innate intelligence. He guessed everyone believed she'd be a hell of a nurse, like her mother wanted. Flathead and Curry had said she was smart, and according to the yearbook, she'd been in the Honor Society. She'd also been on the girls' basketball team and, in her junior year, had been in the Thespians.

No academic, athletic, or extracurricular credits were listed under her son's name in 1966. He had won one distinction, however: "Best-Looking Boy." With his dark eyes and long dark hair, it wasn't hard to see why. Like the other boys, he wore a dark suit and tie in his photo, but the hair seemed to cry out, *Don't let the Sunday clothes fool you.* Harter imagined Roger had a sort of wild appeal to the girls of 1966.

"I see you've found what you were after," said Mrs. Robbins, taking a seat next to him. "They're settled down out there for a while. At least, they're pretending to copy things out of encyclopedias."

"Do you remember Roger Wilton?" Harter asked.

"I think so." She slid the yearbook over in front of her and glanced down at the picture. "You realize, I've never seen students every day, like their regular teachers, and I never learn everyone's name, but I've been racking my brain, and there's something, if this is the right year." She slipped back a few pages. "There she is."

"Who?"

133

"Joyce Dillard. She was my library assistant for a couple of years, and she was crazy about this Wilton boy. Joyce went all moony-eyed over him. They'd walk through the halls hugging and holding hands. I can see myself telling them to separate. You remember the old 'daylight rule,' I guess. But when it came time for the senior prom, the Wilton boy asked someone else. Joyce was awfully upset. They'd argue in the hall and then she'd break into tears."

"You don't recall who he went to the prom with, do you?"

"Yes, I do. That's one more reason why the whole thing sticks in my mind. It was the Malcolm girl. I don't know her first name."

Harter glanced down at Joyce Dillard's photo, then started to turn to the M's in the yearbook.

"Oh, you won't find the other girl there," said Mrs. Robbins. "She didn't attend East Shawnee. She went to the Catholic school, which was odd because her father taught here, or maybe that's why he sent her to parochial school. It's not good for a parent and child, or husband and wife, for that matter, to be in the same school. You may remember her father—Gerald Malcolm."

"He taught me algebra," said Harter. "Is he retired?"

"Six or seven years ago."

"I wonder where his daughter is."

"She's dead," said Mrs. Robbins.

"When?"

"If I'm right, it would have been a year or two before Gerald retired. Tragic. Some devastating illness. She was still in her twenties. She'd been living in California for years. San Francisco, I believe. Gerald never talked about her much. I think he was hurt that she never came back home."

"Strange," said Harter. "You know, Roger Wilton took off

134

for somewhere, maybe California, early in 1968. What about this Joyce Dillard? What ever became of her?"

"Oh, she's easy to locate. She's a librarian at the community college." Mrs. Robbins smiled. "I suppose we sometimes influence our students in a positive way. Joyce is married now. Her husband is a professor. She's Joyce Bertoia now."

"I'll look her up. I have to go out to the campus anyway. Roger Wilton was a student there until just before he left Shawnee."

"Of course, this may all mean nothing."

"That's the way it always is."

"Mrs. Robbins—" A girl in a blue sweater and jeans stood in the doorway to the office. "Would you help me?"

"I'll be back in a minute," the librarian told him as she got up to follow the girl out into the main room.

Harter turned the yearbook pages as he thought about what she'd said. Roger was involved with a girl who'd also headed to California in the sixties. But that meant they weren't her bones in Egypt Street. Nor were they Joyce Dillard's. Hell, the Best-Looking Boy probably had girlfriends aplenty.

He slowly turned his head from Nan Nash to Roger Wilton, from mother to son. They looked a lot alike, and they were both dead.

··· 21 ···

The halls were nearly empty by the time Harter finished with the biology teacher. Mr. Webster had always given off the aura that he was floating above it all, and the vibrations had gotten stronger over the years. Not only didn't he recall Roger Wilton, or Harter for that matter, but you could almost believe he didn't even have a memory of Gerald Malcolm, a man he'd taught with for a couple of decades.

But then, Harter could remember Webster puttering around the science lab on his free periods, so maybe his distance from the rest of East Shawnee High wasn't fabricated. Maybe it was real. Day after day, year after year, he'd carried his thermos and his lunch in a brown sack, so he hadn't gone to the teacher's lounge for coffee or to the cafeteria for food. He'd just never been privy to any of the school gossip.

Yearbooks for 1941 and 1966 were under Harter's arm as he left the building. Mrs. Robbins had said, sure, he could borrow them, though he didn't exactly know why he'd asked. Like the transcript he'd picked up at the principal's office, he didn't know what good they'd be. The stuff certainly wasn't hard evidence. Still, collecting it all made him feel like he was laboring away, and all the paper and the photos gave him something to stare at, something to concentrate on while he tried to think. Hard work, as he'd told Dave McManaway. Not digging in the mud, but hard labor nonetheless.

He climbed in his car, dropped the yearbooks and transcript on the seat next to him, and, before turning the ignition, reached for a cigarette. He was puffing on the thing when, a block from the high school, he passed the alley. A bunch of boys were congregated there off the main street, lighting cigarettes now that their school day was over. He, too, had had his first smoke in that alley on the way down the hill. He'd stood there and felt the dizziness hit his head, the dizziness that only comes when you don't smoke regularly. That, and the feeling of daring.

He rubbed his cigarette out in the ashtray. The damn thing didn't taste so good anymore. Liz was always after him to quit. Maybe he would.

Or maybe those boys weren't smoking tobacco. Maybe they were getting their dizziness some other way. Mr. Adams had mentioned "the turmoil," and how he'd preferred the days when you didn't have to patrol lavatories to find pot smokers. There'd been no marijuana when Harter was in school—none available in Shawnee that he'd known of. Those were the Eisenhower fifties, days of Elvis "Jailhouse Rock," Chuck Berry "Rock and Roll Music," Carl Perkins "Blue Suede Shoes," not heavy metal, not "Mind Games," not psychedelia, no matter how threatening the music had seemed at the time.

But Shawnee in the 1950s hadn't been like "Ozzie and Harriet" either, or "Father Knows Best," or any of those neat, clean TV shows. Those television families had always seemed to live in comfortable households where Dad left each morning in a tie and white shirt and returned undisheveled with a smile and a bit of wisdom. Where the trains didn't rumble through. Where the garbage men didn't rattle the trash-can lids at six in the morning. Where there wasn't even any garbage for them to pick up. Where no one worried how to pay the bills. Where Mom cooked breakfast on a modern range, cleaned house in high heels, went to Ladies Club luncheons, and was there with milk and cookies when the kids came home. Harter had never lived in such a world.

Nor had Roger Wilton, he realized.

Roger, growing up in Shantytown, spoiled or not, must have survived his share of troubles. And even if he turned into a hippie in 1966 and 1967, Roger had also been a kid in the fifties. Younger than Harter, younger than his sister Dorothy, probably more rebellious, arguing with his father. But Harter had, too. Fifties slide into sixties, with no one completely understanding how people change. *Times change*, Flathead Nash had said. Sixties slide into seventies, and seventies into eighties. People age. They fall in and out of love. Kids smoking in alleys become middle-aged men with habits. Stations turn into museums. Floodwaters rise and fall. Bare bones surface. Strange homecomings.

Harter lit another cigarette.

● ● ●

McManaway had gone for the day by the time Harter walked into headquarters. Just as well. He didn't really want to talk.

His desk was becoming so cluttered that he had to push junk aside to make room for the transcript and yearbooks. There were notes from McManaway, a copy of Caruthers' report on the 1967 hit-and-run, Roger Wilton's autopsy, a summary of the findings about the girl's bones, a half-moon earring, a printout from North Carolina on the Subaru, assorted photos, newspaper clippings, a cassette tape, a tape recorder, and a pile of messages from the flurry of phone calls.

Apart from some hamburger wrappers and a few road maps, nothing had been found in Roger's car, according to one of McManaway's notes. The car, by the way, had no tape player and its radio didn't work, McManaway had added as an afterthought. Roger Wilton had purchased the Subaru used in 1983. McManaway still hadn't turned up any criminal record on him or on any of the other people Harter had asked him to check out.

The note attached to Caruthers' report on the death of Nan Wilton said McManaway had read the report again and had no new thoughts.

Pete Epstein's autopsy on Roger didn't contribute much either. Wilton had, indeed, been shot twice in the chest, as Epstein had said on Sunday morning. The time was estimated as shortly after nine o'clock on Saturday night. Epstein still believed the shooting had taken place somewhere else and the body simply dumped behind the picnic table on Black's Mountain.

The university expert hadn't been back in touch with anything about the bones.

For what it was worth, the earring was probably untraceable after all these years.

The tape didn't have anything on it other than what they'd heard in the motel room that morning. McManaway had made copies and had sent one to Sergeant Smith, who, by the way, hadn't communicated anything new or startling. No one had called with anything worth repeating, either.

From the clipped tone of McManaway's scribbles, Harter could tell the younger cop was beginning to wear down from crossing t's and dotting i's. And he'd been the one who'd left those *t*'s uncrossed and those *i*'s undotted, the one who'd left it up to McManaway to copy it all over in ink. Thankless job, but you had to learn some way, he told himself. Someone had to deal with the technical fine points while someone else mined the people. Mining the people in a case was usually pretty untechnical, unscientific. Maybe that was why Harter liked it. Fingerprints, tire marks, autopsies only took you so far. He just hoped Dave McManaway wouldn't come to hate him, as, over the years, he himself had come to hate Caruthers.

Only time and experience could teach you some things. Even then, you often worked in the dark. It was like when he was young and telling his father or his grandfather about some problem or worry, and when they looked back at him he could see the baffled expressions on their faces, the expressions that said they were lost, too. No "Father Knows Best."

He picked up the cassette tape and slid it into the tape player. Soon he was hearing Roger's soft voice.

What the fuck am I doing   Didn't want to do it then either   Just talking into this damn box   Trying to get my thoughts ordered   Hard to line all the ducks in a row   Didn't know what to do that night either   Nineteen sixty-seven   Mom   In the shed   Lucky the old man was away   They'd called him out to a train wreck in the country someplace and he was gone every night that week   We knew we had to do it then   The old bastard never would have understood   He'd have climbed on his high horse   Mom said it wasn't good but it was right   She promised to help so   it didn't happen to me what—

And then a truck outside the Goodnight Motel blotted out whatever "what" was.

• • •

It didn't happen to me what—

... 22 ...

Next morning it was all in the newspapers in the minutest detail. It even had additions—consisting of Detective This, Detective That, and Detective The Other's "Theory" as to how the robbery was done, who the robbers were, and whither they had flown with their booty. There were eleven of these theories, and they covered all the possibilities; and this single fact shows what independent thinkers detectives are. No two theories were alike, or even much resembled each other, save in one striking particular, and in that one all the eleven theories were absolutely agreed. That was, that although the rear of my building was torn out and the only door remained locked, the elephant had not been removed through the rent, but by some other (undiscovered) outlet. All agreed that the robbers had made that rent only to mislead the detectives. That never would have occurred to me or to any other layman, perhaps, but it had not deceived the detectives for a moment. Thus, what I had supposed was the only thing that had no mystery about it was in fact the very thing I had gone furthest astray in.

He had read Mark Twain's story "The Stolen White Elephant" many times, Samuel Clemens fan that he was. He'd read the tale in cabooses as trains powered along, chuckling over the humorous account of the search for a missing pachyderm. After he got off the phone with Flathead Nash, Curry had pulled the battered old book off the parlor shelf and flipped through the dog-eared pages for Twain's yarn. He'd hoped the story would make him feel better about how detectives went about their business, how their minds worked, what they were apt to miss. He'd hoped the tale would make him feel better, but it didn't. The words tended to swim in front of his tired, dark eyes. Instead of making him relax, they made him realize even more that what was going on wasn't humor or satire, wasn't some fiction about inept dicks and an elephant, wasn't something to laugh about. It was a tragedy.

The bones, the death of Nan, now the killing of the boy. No humor, only tragedy. Not tall-tale stuff. *Real*. As real as the floodwater lapping at his porch steps, leaving the guts of his house damp and chill.

Harter wasn't Detective This, or Detective That, or Detective The Other, loaded down with crazy theories. He was a hard-nosed cop and what he might find scared the old man.

"What'd he want to know?" Curry had asked Flathead on the phone.

"Mostly about Nan and the boy. He wasn't here all that long."

"What'd you tell him?"

"That I wasn't around when none of it happened."

Which was true as far as it went. Flathead usually told the truth, within his limits.

The boy. Who'd have figured Roger would come back to Shawnee? Who'd have figured?

Curry looked out the window, over at the Wilton place, just across Egypt Street, not very far, though sometimes it had seemed so distant, like the night Nan had crossed—had *tried* to cross. She'd only been crossing the street. She shouldn't have been in danger. There should have been something he could have done to save her. He hadn't even heard it.

Outside, the darkness was almost complete. It was cloudy again. He hoped it wouldn't rain.

His eyes returned to the book on his lap. He turned back to the start of Twain's elephant saga.

The following curious history was related to me by a chance railway acquaintance. He was a gentleman more than seventy years of age, and his thoroughly good and gentle face and earnest and sincere manner imprinted the unmistakable stamp of truth upon every statement which fell from his lips.

He hoped that was how Harter saw him: thoroughly good, gentle, earnest, sincere, truthful. That there could be more to him, or anyone, was beside the point. For the time being, it was all what people—*what Harter*—believed. If the cop dug too deep, it couldn't help anyone.

Curry closed the book, tossed it over on the daybed, pushed himself up from his soft chair. He commanded his stiff legs to maneuver the stairs to his bedroom, and once he got there, he pulled open a dresser drawer with some difficulty. The drawer was as affected by dampness, as temperamental, as arthritic, as hard to move as his legs. He rooted around until he found the box, then lifted it out, placed it on top of the dresser, and removed the lid. His clumsy fingers sifted through the small pieces—the cufflinks that had belonged to his father before he'd disappeared, the wedding ring that had been his mother's, the tiepin he'd worn as a young man, the earring, all knots on a long heavy rope that twisted its way back into the past. Tug on the rope and it was like you were pulling the past into the present, all those knots linked together like boxcars and gondolas on a freight train stretched long on the tracks through the mountains, ready to wreck if something went wrong, pennies on a rail. *Falling rock.* Old men argue. After a while, he and Wheat were no longer those two close friends playing among canal boat hulls, and Egypt Street grew wider between their houses, until sometimes it was like the Red Sea and you needed God himself to part the waters so you could get across. *Pharaoh's army got drown-ded.* But, no, it had been Nan who drowned.

He stared down at the earring in his hand. He'd known the night he found it that it wasn't hers, so he'd picked it up, put it in his pocket, and later he hid it in his drawer. *December 1967.* The night after she'd died. Wheat and Roger had been at the funeral home and Curry had wandered over and circled the Wilton house, taking it in, as if he'd never see the place again, even though it was directly across the street from him.

He'd opened the shed to see if the floor looked too disturbed, too suspicious, and he'd spotted the earring, a half-moon of a thing. He'd known it wasn't Nan's. Her ears weren't pierced, and when she wore jewelry, she liked it to sparkle. She liked jewelry that sparkled, like her eyes, and the earring didn't.

Still holding it, he sat on the corner of his bed. The earring couldn't have done anyone any good—and couldn't now. It would just ruin reputations, memories. Nan had told him about the girl the night it happened, just two nights before she herself was hit by the truck. God, there should have been something he could have done.

They'd been lying on the bed, this bed, and she'd told him what had happened, just as she'd told him so many things over the years. And, as she'd done so often, she pledged him to secrecy. He'd tried not to show his shock, tried not to quote Bible verses like his mother would have, tried to accept her confession with grace.

She was upset, and he'd reached over and put his arm around her. They'd been fully clothed, and she was worn out

144

and upset from burying the girl. Lying on the bed, fully dressed, talking serious. Sometimes it had been like that. And other times . . .

She hadn't expected, hadn't wanted, it to happen like it did. She'd only had the best intentions. He'd put his arm around her and told her, yes, he believed her. He didn't believe Nan and Roger would murder anyone. It was the times. And now, these times, these years later, there was no sense muddying names, not hers. Harter would have to sort it out by himself. He'd pledged himself to secrecy.

He'd broken that pledge only once. Flathead had come to Egypt Street once, months later—drunk, as he often was. Drunk and angry, ready to beat someone up. Down in his cups over the killing of his sister. Filled with his own theories about what had happened, just like those eleven detectives with their wild theories about the missing elephant. It had been soon after Roger had left town to escape Wheat, and Flathead was sure the boy had something to do with it. He ranted about going to the police. He ranted about Wheat. Finally, Curry had gotten him calmed a trifle, had sat him down, poured some coffee down his throat, and then he'd told him what he knew, what Nan had confessed. He knew Flathead wouldn't do anything to hurt his sister. Even in his craziest moments, Flathead loved his sister. So it became a secret two men shared, and now someone else was digging for it. Roger hadn't helped by coming back to Shawnee. He'd only added more shovels.

He could see the cops over behind Nan's house the week before, digging up the bones. He could see Harter crossing the street toward him for the first visit on Wednesday morning. Like Nan had so many times. Those years of crossing Egypt Street at night, at odd hours, when Wheat was away working a wreck or some job, when Curry and Nan could arrange the time without raising eyebrows. All those times, knots in a long heavy rope, he could almost feel them still. Falling rocks, and the mountains change shape.

The first time was so long ago, he couldn't recall. You'd think you'd remember the first time, but he really couldn't. It had just come about slow and natural, a word dropped here, a glance there, and then she'd started walking over with a piece of pie or cookies, and then she was telling Curry it should have been him she married in 1942, and not Wheat. The years went by, and first Wheat argued with him about any subject that came up, and then they stopped talking altogether. They would never again build a shed together.

He could see her standing by the dresser, near the bed, unbuttoning the front of her dress, then sliding the dress from her shoulders, and after it dropped down her body to the floor, she bent her knee to lift her foot free of it. In her white lace-edged slip, she came over to him, her arms reaching out, and his to hers. He pulled her down on top of him and rubbed at her smooth back, down to her buttocks. Never could have imagined it. There'd been a time he never could have imagined it. When he'd thought he'd lost her for good. So soft against his hard. She never seemed to age. She was always as attractive to him as she'd been when he first saw her in the thin summer dress with the high heels strapped across her ankles at the bus stop that warm day, 1941. Always that attractive to him, year after year.

He'd never do anything to hurt her.

··· 23 ···

Harter turned the corner at the SHAWNEE COMMUNITY COL-
LEGE sign and drove past a baseball field, unused this November
morning. Ahead of him, the hollow between the ridges was
filled with a complex of red brick buildings and parking lots.
Built in the early sixties for a small student population, the tiny
college with no dormitories had always struck him as little more
than a glorified high school. Still, before Shawnee Community,
there'd been no place in town for anyone to get any sort of
"higher education."

In the early 1970s, when the powers-that-be had decided
cops should be more humane and well rounded, Harter had attended night courses in sociology, psychology, and criminology
in the main building. The classes had by and large been junk,
and he'd kept finding himself believing he was back at East
Shawnee High. He bet many of the kids on campus developed
the same feeling. Roger Wilton, Class A rebel, probably had.

He parked near the student union and debated whether to
go inside for another cup of coffee before hitting the registrar's
office and the library. It had been in the student center one
night that he'd met Liz. Then, as now, she was a part-time
instructor in dance and exercise. Teaching a few mornings and

147

evenings at the community college was about the only way she, or anyone else, could eke out a living giving dance lessons in Shawnee. Her studio on the West Side certainly couldn't pay for itself. Sometimes he wondered if she ever had second thoughts about moving back from New York City.

He decided against an umpteenth cup of coffee. He didn't need it, and there was no point in taking the chance of running into Liz. Tuesday morning was one of the times she was likely to be on campus, and he wondered if that wasn't why he'd picked this time to come.

She was still on his mind when he showed his badge to the woman in the registrar's office and requested whatever info they had on Roger Wilton, for whatever good it was. The secretary was obviously not one who'd been there eighteen years before, and there was no reason why she'd remember Roger even if she had been.

Roger had enrolled in 1966, the fall after he'd graduated from high school, according to the transcript Harter was given. He'd attended classes for a year and a half, until January 1968, and there the trail ended. His courses were a mishmash. Some he'd dropped, others he'd failed, and if he'd been a success at anything, it had been a freshman writing course where he'd gotten a B. His final semester had been a real washout, but Harter guessed that was to be expected. Roger had apparently been turning hippier and hippier, and, after all, he must have been affected by the death of his mother in December, not to mention whatever else had happened. During his last days at Shawnee Community College, he might even have been planning his own disappearance. Draft calls would have been high in 1967–68, and Harter wondered whether Roger bothered to inform the Selective Service of his cutting out.

He folded the copy of the transcript, stuck it in his jacket pocket, and left the administration building. Outside, students and professors rushed about him as he plowed on to the library. Up ahead, he spotted a woman in black tights. She had short, dark hair and a dancer's body. At first he was convinced she was Liz, and he didn't know whether to speed up to catch her or slow down to avoid her. On second look, he noticed she was young and her hair was teased up and had a red streak through it. She wore a slick gold jacket covered with crazy pins and patches, and barely sticking out below the jacket was the fringe of a short, short red skirt. She had on spike heels, not dancing shoes. If she'd worn such an outfit to East Shawnee High when he'd been a student, *before the turmoil*, the principal would have shipped her home for a haircombing and more ladylike attire, like Mr. Adams wished he still could.

Hell, there was no reason she shouldn't show off those legs. Girls would wear whatever they thought would attract boys, and this one must earn a lot of glances. Enough years of being a responsible adult stretched gray and long in front of her, thought Harter.

She turned up the sidewalk to the library and he followed. She wasn't very used to the tall, thin heels and wobbled a little as she negotiated the steps. Inside, she went over to a table where two other girls with wild hair and heavily made-up eyes sat with a mass of papers and books spread out before them. Harter walked to the desk and asked about Joyce Dillard, class of 1966.

Joyce Dillard Bertoia seemed upset that a detective had come to see her at work. It was like she feared he'd lead her out of the library in handcuffs while students formed a gauntlet all the way to the paddy wagon. She didn't look much like her picture in the old yearbook. She'd be thirty-six or thirty-seven now, and with her hair pulled back and a skirt that dropped nearly to her ankles, it was hard to picture her as a boy-struck teenager clutching Roger Wilton in the hall, as Mrs. Robbins had described.

Her blue eyes scanned the room as they talked, and eventually she led him back to a storage room loaded with books on shelves and in crates. Harter didn't need a Ph.D. in psychology to grasp that she didn't want to discuss Roger. Yes, she'd read about his death, but she knew nothing, she said. And he believed her.

"I don't know why you came to see me. I've not seen him since before he left Shawnee," she insisted.

"I understand you used to date him. I'm interested in who he knew back then. It's a long shot, but I figure he must have looked up some old friends after he came back. There has to be a reason for his return."

"Don't you think it had something to do with the skeleton they found last week? I read about that, too."

"We figure it most likely does."

"Well, he certainly didn't come to visit me," she said. "We stopped dating in high school. He was getting pretty weird."

"What do you mean—*weird*?"

"Weird . . . Not normal . . . But I didn't actually see it very clearly at the time. It was hard to see things clearly in the Nineteen sixties."

"You mean he took drugs?"

"No, not in high school. Not when he was around me, at least. Maybe later—I imagine he did later. What I mean is that he acted weird, did lunatic things at times. You couldn't predict him. Like the time—"

"What time?"

Mrs. Bertoia looked down at her lap. The fingers of her right hand were nervously twisting her wedding ring around and around.

"One night in a cemetery . . ." She shook her head.

150

"Come on. Tell me about it."

"It was the fall we were going together. The fall before we graduated. There was some crazy story about how a statue in a cemetery moved, and he got the idea he wanted to see it. We'd been to a Halloween party, and then we drove out in the country to the graveyard."

"And?"

"Roger would get these things in his head. He was convinced that if the statue really did move, it would be at midnight on Halloween. When we got out there, we had to walk quite a distance through the grave markers and all. I was dressed up for the party, and my shoes kept sticking in the mud. He had a flashlight, and he'd shine it ahead of us. Finally we came to this memorial, this angel sitting on a chair—a throne, I guess—over a grave. He told me to sit in its lap and—this is painful, Mr. Harter—"

"And you sat on the statue?"

She nodded. "I wanted him to sit there first, but he said the thing only moved when a girl sat on its lap. I'd have done almost anything for him. I was so dumb in those days. After I sat down, he switched off the flashlight and we stayed there in the dark awhile. I remember the concrete was cold against the backs of my legs, and after a few minutes I told him I wanted to leave. But he didn't answer. I told him again that I'd had enough of this silliness, but he didn't even seem to be there. I got scared, sitting on the grave, the clamminess and all, and I started screaming, but there was no sign of him. I jumped up and started running. It was dark, and I kept tripping and falling in the mud. I rammed into a tombstone and ripped my nylons— Why am I telling you this?—"

"You're honest, and I asked."

"Some animal was howling in the woods. I thought it was a wildcat. I took off my shoes so I could run better, but I kept running into headstones, like the graves were a maze. When I got back to the car, it was all locked up and I didn't know what to do. I just stood there, no shoes, my feet and stockings wet and dirty, my clothes muddy and torn, crying, wailing. Then Roger leaped out of the bushes and yelled *Boo!* and laughed and—"

"Nice guy."

"He could be," she said, suddenly defensive, as if she'd bared too much. "I can't begin to explain, but if he'd asked me to go out there with him again the next week, I probably would have. I told you I was dumb in those days."

"You dated him for quite a while after the scene in the graveyard, didn't you?"

"We went together until spring, when he—when he met someone else."

"A Malcolm girl? The daughter of Mr. Malcolm, the high school teacher?"

"Yes."

"Did you know her?"

"Not really, but from what I saw she was more like Roger than I was. More in his line. She was willing to do anything."

"What do you mean?" asked Harter, though he knew the question was touchy.

"I . . . I don't really know what went on between them, Mr. Harter. I wouldn't want to guess. Talk to her."

"I can't. She's dead."

"Oh—I didn't know."

"I'm going to see her parents, in case they remember anything."

"Mr. Malcolm always seemed like a kind man," said Mrs. Bertoia, apparently happy to change the subject.

"Yeah, he did. How about anyone else—maybe a friend Roger might have looked up when he came back here last week?"

"I'm at a loss. I don't know. Possibly Len."

"Who's he?"

"Len Schiller."

"The guy in his thirties who lives over on Billings Street?"

She shrugged. "I don't keep in contact with him, or with most people from those days. Len had dropped out of high school and had an apartment. We'd go visit him sometimes. Do you know him?"

"I've busted him. Possession and burglary. Couldn't pin anything more on him, though he always seems to be around trouble."

"After Roger and I broke up, he was with Len Schiller or Christy Malcolm almost every time I'd run into him. He wasn't one to have a lot of close friends. Only a couple at a time."

"I'll check Schiller out. How about Roger's parents? Did you ever meet them?"

"I met his mother a few times. She was just about the only person he'd listen to at all, but she wasn't one to come down on him hard."

"So I've heard. How about his father?"

"He hardly ever mentioned his father, as I recall."

"Look, if something else pops into your mind, give me a call. You've been a lot of help."

"I hope nothing else pops into my mind," she said, showing a sliver of a smile for the first time. He supposed Joyce Bertoia could relax now that he was leaving.

She was chatting with another librarian at the front counter when he went out the library door. The other woman might be asking her why a cop had come to see her. If so, Harter was sure she wasn't having a lot of fun explaining. It wouldn't be much more pleasant than sitting in the lap of a cold, clammy, grave-guarding angel on a black Halloween night, waiting for the statue to move. Might even be a similar wrenching experience for her. Sometimes it was hard to tell the quick from the dead.

He was opening his car door when he saw Liz strolling across the parking lot to her car. Swinging her tote bag, her dancer's legs striding, her dark hair blowing a bit, she looked carefree as hell. He started to walk over to her, then froze. So carefree, in a way he never could seem to be.

She hadn't spotted him, so he climbed in the car and turned the key. He was two cars behind her when she pulled off campus and onto the highway back to town. As they braked for the second traffic light, a blue Shawnee-Potomac Railroad truck swung in ahead of him, adding another length between them.

The light changed, and Liz turned right, toward her studio and her afternoon aerobics class for the West Side Women's Club. The blue railroad truck swung left and Harter followed. First, he would visit Gerald Malcolm to see where that track went, and then he would find Len Schiller and see what the punk had to offer. Maybe, after that, he could be carefree. Maybe he would go see Liz.

··· 24 ···

Gerald Malcolm lived just off the Old Pennsylvania Pike on the north side of Shawnee in a white house that, once upon a time, had obviously been the center of a prosperous farm. Now a string of new brick and aluminum-sided residences lined the road into the place, but behind the retired teacher's home, a red barn still rose up tall from an antique stone foundation. Harter parked beside a green pickup truck and, walking toward the front porch, noticed that the barn and the large garden plot nearby looked like they were in active use. He wasn't much of a farm boy, but he'd seen enough apple trees to recognize a small orchard on the hillside. It, too, appeared to be well tended.

Malcolm exuded cheeriness when Harter introduced himself, former student to former algebra instructor. They chatted noncommittally for a few minutes about East Shawnee High School, and then Mr. Malcolm's smile turned down and his lips slammed shut as soon as Harter informed him he was a cop and explained why he'd come. Like Joyce Bertoia, Malcolm seemed surprised, even shocked. Or maybe, thought Harter, he was misinterpreting the expression. Maybe the mention of Christy Malcolm had brought back a pain her father had fought hard to get over.

Finally, uncomfortably, Malcolm invited him in. A few steps inside, he started to lead Harter through a doorway to the living room, then froze, as if he was tossed up about which room to use. The girl on the couch was confused, too. She dropped her magazine on the coffee table and stood up like she was about to leave the room to them. She was black, maybe sixteen or seventeen, and her swollen belly pressed tight against an oversize T-shirt.

"Just someone to see me, Karen," said Malcolm, motioning her back to the couch. Then he led Harter down the hall and into a sort of office.

The room was clearly divided in halves, and Harter got the impression it was probably the most-used room in the house. Malcolm's age showed as he dropped into a swivel chair beside an old-fashioned rolltop desk. The top was open and Harter could see that each of the desk's cubbyholes was crammed with letters, bills, and what looked like agricultural publications. "This your farm office?" he asked.

Malcolm ran his hand back over his bald head. The hand, his arm, was big, still looked strong. "Farming is a losing proposition, but it gives me something to do. I sold some of the land for development years ago, but I kept fifty acres. That's more than I can handle. Sit down, Ed—*Detective*."

Harter did, and leaned his arm on the edge of a gray metal desk, much like the one he dreaded in his own office. The flat surface was as full of papers, mail, and magazines as the rolltop desk across the room. Amid the clutter, Harter spotted a big sheet of tagboard next to Magic Markers of different colors. Someone had started to print a poster but hadn't gotten any farther than BENEFIT in red block letters.

"My wife," said Malcolm.

"Your wife?"

"The poster you're staring at. That's her project. You've

probably never met Connie, but that's how she spends her days."

"What's the benefit for?"

"The Allegheny Unwed Mothers' Home. Connie does volunteer work for them. Sometimes she puts in forty or fifty hours a week."

"Sounds like a worthwhile cause," said Harter, happy to give Malcolm his head for a while, happy to let him talk about anything he wanted, hoping the talk would relax him.

"Quite worthwhile, I'd say, and important. Every young woman who carries her baby full-term means one who doesn't turn to abortion. That's the main thing to us. That's how Connie got involved with the home. She's Catholic, you understand, and takes it very seriously. I'm not myself, but we always sent our daughter to parochial school for the strong moral background. Anyway, Connie joined the local Right to Life chapter years ago, and she's gone to Washington for demonstrations and all. She was always angry over all those babies being aborted, murdered. After Christy's death, she became even more aware of the children who aren't allowed to be born, and of the people who want kids but can't find one. That led her to work with the home for unwed mothers. When they have more young women than they can handle, we keep some of them here."

"Like the girl in the living room?"

"Yes. Like Karen. I suppose the most we ever took in at one time was three, and that was some houseful, I'll tell you. But it does Connie a world of good to help the girls through their rough spots. The girls become like daughters to us, like the daughter we lost at such a young age. We grow attached to some of them, and they write us for years afterwards. And it keeps Connie sane."

"I guess the babies are put up for adoption, huh?"

"In most cases. Oh, a few girls decide to keep their babies, but mostly they're adopted out. There are so many couples unable to have children, Detective. There's quite a waiting list, though it's a shame that sometimes it's hard to place black babies. The Allegheny Home takes care of everything. They think they've found a family for Karen's, which is just in the nick of time. She's due in a month. That's where Connie is right now. She often visits the adopting families beforehand to be sure they're the right kind of people."

"Sounds like good work," said Harter, his mind drifting . . . somewhere else . . . to McManaway . . . Dave and Sally . . . about to have a baby they wanted . . . no abortions, no adoptions, no problems.

"We try to do good works."

Harter stared over at the ex-teacher and tried to look through Malcolm's glasses, through the thick lenses, at his eyes. He felt like a jerk when he pulled the conversation back on the road. "I guess I can understand your wife's dedication. Your daughter *was* young when she died, wasn't she?"

"Twenty-eight. It was in March Nineteen seventy-eight, just two months before her twenty-ninth birthday."

"She died from—"

"A brain tumor. No one knew she had it until it was too late."

"And she was living in San Francisco?"

"Yes. Christy moved out there the fall after she graduated from high school. She attended college there and liked the West Coast so well that she decided to stay."

"You must have made a number of trips out there over the years, especially when she was ill."

"Not enough, I'm afraid. Not as many as we should have. I'd say that's part of the reason for some of the emptiness that . . . that Connie is trying to overcome. It's hard on mothers to lose their children. Connie says that after abortions, some women even find themselves mourning for the aborted fetus they never saw. It's even harder when you're not prepared for the death. As I said, Christy didn't know about the tumor until it was too late. She informed us only a week before she died. She was like that—quite independent."

"Was she married?"

"No. She'd thrown everything into her career. She worked for an investment firm out there. Had a bright future."

"She'd have graduated here in, what, Nineteen sixty-six?"

"It was 'sixty-seven, actually."

"Then she was a year younger than Roger Wilton?"

"I believe so."

"And she left for California early in Nineteen sixty-eight, about the same time he did?"

"No. It wasn't like that at all." Malcolm took off his thick glasses and placed them on the desk. Turning back to Harter, he squinted and said, "If you want the truth, Christy went to California to get away from the Wilton boy. Believe me, that was the only reason Connie and I would have allowed her to go out there on her own. We were quite protective parents when she was at home."

"Why did she have to get away from him?"

"They'd broken up, which made Connie and me happy, but he wouldn't stop calling her at all hours. More than once, he sat in a car at the end of the driveway and waited for her to go to work or go out. If you're suggesting she ran away with him, you're dead wrong, Detective. She had the good sense to want to free herself from a bad influence."

"You and your wife didn't approve of Roger Wilton?"

"That was no secret."

"Any particular reason?"

"He was wild, had no standards. And from what we learned of the family, they weren't the best, either."

"He was a hippie and your daughter found him attractive?"

"You could put it like that."

"You know, in Nineteen sixty-seven, San Francisco was known as the hippie capital of the world. Is that why she wanted to move out there?"

"I've already explained. Christy went to college there. She spent the summer and fall of 'sixty-seven here in Shawnee, working at a store downtown and saving money for college. Just after Thanksgiving, she flew out to San Francisco so she could get situated for the second semester. Connie and I went out at Christmas to see her apartment and spend the holidays with her. I have no idea why the Wilton boy ran off to California—*if he did*. But if it was to find Christy, he must have been disappointed. She never mentioned him again." Malcolm put his glasses back on, but the thick lenses couldn't cover up the anger shooting from his eyes. "Are you investigating my daughter, Detective, or are you investigating the murder of Roger Wilton? Which is it?"

"I'm sorry."

The words came out like a reflex reaction. Over and over, Harter felt the need to apologize. He kept overstepping bounds, digging into private tender spots that didn't, on the surface, have much to do with the case. He'd already done it that day with Joyce Bertoia, and he'd done it on Sunday with Dorothy Merrill, and maybe he'd even done it with Matt Curry. Then, there'd been Paul Keith, the gentleman from Pittsburgh who'd lost track of his wife during World War II. Seemed like so long ago that Keith had called him, but it had actually been less than a week. Some cases were like that—sometimes you seemed to rough up people's emotions. He hoped no one would ever force him to give a good reason why.

Karen, the pregnant black girl, watched nervously as he passed the living room on his way to the front door. Gerald

160

Malcolm stood on the porch and looked glad as hell when Harter started out the driveway.

He was almost to the road when a beige station wagon pulled in toward him. He glanced over and saw a round-faced woman with gray hair in the driver's seat. He figured she was Connie Malcolm and, for a second, it seemed like she was about to roll down her window and say something to him, but instead she edged on past. In his rearview mirror, he could see the bumper sticker on the back of her station wagon.

SAVE THE BABIES

He could picture Mrs. Malcolm going into the farmhouse and then into the office to finish the poster for the Allegheny Unwed Mothers Home. He pictured her grieving for her daughter and trying to work out her grief by throwing herself into a cause.

Why the hell did he keep bulldozing over good people?

At least when he found Roger's old friend Len Schiller he wouldn't have to feel so guilty. Schiller deserved to be flattened out now and again.

··· 25 ···

The first time Harter arrested him, Len Schiller had been standing outside a bar smoking a joint. Harter had been working a car theft and had gone to the tavern to find one of the suspects and take him for a ride.

It had been the early seventies, and the unspoken policy was to bust only dealers and serious drug offenders, not necessarily the guy with the small stash. As Harter had come up the street that night, he'd hadn't earned so much as any eyeball from Schiller. He'd ignored the marijuana smoke and ducked in the bar, but his man wasn't there. When he'd emerged a few minutes later, Schiller was still on the corner, talking to a teenage girl, a fresh joint in his hand, marijuana smoke drifting above his head, cocky as hell, and it was more than Harter could take. So he busted him, amid a lot of squawking about police brutality. Schiller served thirty days for possession.

The second time Harter arrested him, Len Schiller's apartment had looked like a warehouse for stolen goods. He had a TV for every channel and two stereos for every room. Schiller's lawyer had argued that his client had simply bought the hot stuff from other guys and didn't have any notion where it came from. Maybe his client was dumb, maybe he couldn't pass up a good deal, but he was no thief, according to the attorney. Schiller ended up serving five months in the local jail on a plea bargain. He'd told the jailers that he'd needed a rest anyway.

To Harter, Schiller wasn't as goddamn dumb as his lawyer would have it, and he *was* a thief, pure and simple. He was one of those jerks you saw everywhere around town but couldn't quite grasp what they were doing there, or how they made a living. It was hard to pin anything on him that was worth the effort. At some point, you crossed the line into harassment if you stayed on him, or so a shyster would claim.

Back in the sixties, when Roger Wilton would have known him, Schiller might have appeared to be a romantic, outside-the-law hero with long hair and a drooping mustache, but eventually the outlaw streak had deepened and taken over altogether. Harter never saw him any longer in the company of anyone who worked for a paycheck. Over the years, he'd grown grayer, dirtier, tougher. God knows what he'd done or was capable of doing.

Schiller's place on Billings Street was much more than a three-room apartment. He lived in the corner fifth of a huge brick building that ate up an odd triangular city block. Four stories tall, the joint sort of faced west at the tracks and the downtown, in a catty-cornered way. The upper floors had once been rooms for railroad workers while the street level had been lined with shops—a cobbler, a dry cleaner, a ma-and-pa grocery, a liquor store, and others. The structure had been earmarked for demolition in a lame 1960s urban renewal project that mostly fell apart. Aside from Schiller and a tenant at the other end, the building had long been vacant, and the jagged-glass, half-boarded-up windows of the upper stories testified to its uncertain future.

Each time Harter passed the building, he got the inspiration that a movie director could make good use of it. There were plenty of spots around Shawnee like that. Maybe the tourist-seeking town fathers should get in touch with Hollywood. Alfred Hitchcock would have loved the building's menace. Jimmy Stewart would have had a vertigo attack if he'd been forced to climb the winding staircases inside. Hitchcock could have filmed *Psycho* there, too, though it would have been a different movie. No less frightening than the Bates Motel, however. The sprawling Billings Street monster was surely someplace the molemen might hang out, and Len Schiller was surely one of the molemen.

He rapped at the front door, and when no one answered he rapped harder. His pounding seemed to echo off the building across the street. There was no reason for the feeling, but he could have sworn someone was inside. It was just one of those intuitions you get, just one of those inklings that his life often depended on.

He went around the side in time to see a gray van tear up the potholed alley. The back door pushed open from the force of his knock. Schiller, or someone, had been in such a hurry that he hadn't pulled it shut tight. He waited for a minute, then entered, no breaking involved.

The kitchen was as he remembered, though it seemed cleaner and more modern than when he'd last seen it. The outside of the building was deceptive. You expected some poverty-stricken, run-down flat and what you found was a well-equipped, fairly comfortable residence. The microwave oven, refrigerator, and other appliances were pretty new. The walls had been painted in the not-so-distant past, but every inch of space over the kitchen table was still covered with snapshots of Schiller and his friends, pictures torn from magazines and newspapers, posters of rock stars, and a few Playmates of the Month.

Harter wandered into the living room and noted a new rack-system stereo, a large color TV, a videocassette recorder, and other trappings of a middle-class life. Missing was the clutter of obviously stolen goods that he'd found the second time he'd busted Schiller. Nor did there seem to be drugs, baggies, or paraphernalia sitting around.

He opened a door that led to a hallway and steps up to the second floor. Given the immensity of the near-vacant building, he wondered if Schiller was using one of the upstairs rooms for his warehouse, allowing a lawyer to argue that he was totally unaware of what was up there. Harter was about to go up and check it out when he heard the car. He closed the hall door and peeked through the living room curtains.

A Toyota had pulled to the curb and two clean-cut teenagers were climbing out. Harter glanced down at his watch. Three thirty-five. School would have ended a short time before.

The boys made for the front door and he retreated to the kitchen. As he hoped, they knocked rather than walked in. Waiting them out, he leaned on the table and stared at the collage Schiller had put together over the years. Some of the stuff on the wall overlapped other stuff like layers of years, and some of it was faded with age.

The boys stayed at the door a long while, like they were used to Schiller keeping them waiting. Finally, after Harter heard the car engine start up and the Toyota drive up Billings Street, he went out the back door, leaving it slightly ajar.

He was most of the way to headquarters when he decided to make a detour.

• • •

From the overlook, Shawnee didn't look all that different than it had when, as a kid, he'd camped on the mountain with his father. The river and the canal still defended the south side, and the Shawnee-Potomac mainline still cut through the crotch of the city. The big buildings that stood out from a distance were, by and large, the same ones that had always stood out. What had perhaps changed was what went on inside those buildings. What had changed was the people. What had changed was the content, not the form. It was more mental than physical. *Mind games.*

Still, turning west, facing beyond the city toward the high mountains, you could almost believe nothing had changed. Those mountains—from the overlook there were rows of them—mile after mile of Allegheny ridges, blue and occasionally purple. You could only ever see the tops of them, one behind another. Just the very tops. They hid each other, shielded each other from close scrutiny. They prevented anyone from seeing what really went on between them.

... 26 ...

The office was empty when Harter walked in with a hoagie in one hand and, in the other, a Styrofoam cup full of water from the hall cooler. He pushed aside papers and messages to make a spot to eat.

The spicy aroma of salami and olive oil—drenched lettuce burst into the room as he unwrapped the white paper. Caruthers had always accused him of stinking up their office whenever he brought in one of Mattioni's hoagies. So there'd been days when Harter had bought one for the hell of it, just as he'd sometimes blown cigarette smoke Caruthers' way to jag at him. Now Caruthers was in Florida. How long would it take for the edge to wear off, for Harter to erase the former detective from his mind? A while, he suspected.

All around, there were reminders of Caruthers. Like those damn filing cabinets, filled with old cases. Like the 1967 report sitting on the corner of his desk, the report on the death of Nan Wilton. Maybe he should move all the furniture around and clean house to clear away the years of Caruthers. Maybe, one day, he'd even be able to forget the night Caruthers had been slow in coming to his rescue after a cane-wielding madman had disarmed him with a blow from his weighted stick. Dave McManaway just had to be better.

He took another bite of hoagie and sifted through Tuesday's accumulation of paper. On top was a note from McManaway: "Call me at home. You won't believe this." He decided to put off the call until he was done eating.

Another note informed him that Sergeant Wayne Smith had been in touch. The state police were giving up on the North Carolina angle. They hadn't turned up so much as a hint that Roger's murder had anything to do with anyone down there.

Then there was the morning's newspaper, which Harter hadn't bothered to read before he'd headed out to Shawnee Community College. The brief item in the local section reported only that Roger's car had been found near the high school and police continued to investigate the case. There was no mention of the Goodnight Motel or other details. McManaway had obviously been choosy about the facts he gave out. Score another one for Dave.

Finally, there was a fingerprint report with yet another note paper-clipped to it. McManaway had saved him the trouble of reading the entire thing by summarizing: "Roger Wilton's were the only prints found in the motel room or the Subaru." Harter skimmed the report anyway.

All this paper, all this work, to find out who murdered a guy no one particularly cared about. To identify some bones that were nearly twenty years old. Maybe, to delve back into a 1967 hit-and-run. *Christ.*

But you couldn't look at it that way. No one had the right to go around shooting people, or to bury bodies in the backyard, or to run people down. And whoever had done those things might still be walking Shawnee streets. Or the whoevers—the *whoevers* who'd done them.

He balled up the hoagie wrapper and tossed it at the trash can, then reached for the phone. Sally McManaway sounded cheery as hell when she answered. He tried to be equally upbeat. "How you doing, Sally?"

"Fine."

"No labor pains?"

"Not yet, but we're getting down to the last few days."

"Dave's told me. I suppose you have a bag all packed and waiting by the door."

"Oh, a brand-new one. Dave bought it for me." She laughed. "He keeps coming home with all sorts of things. He even bought pickles and ice cream. But there must be something wrong with me. I don't have a craving for them, and they just sit in the refrigerator. Do you want to talk to him?"

"Unless the two of you are in the middle of a practice run to the hospital."

"We've already done that. I'll get him."

Harter heard the bump of the phone against a table. As he waited, he wished he'd had more to say to her, something more than small talk. But he really didn't know her that well, and babies weren't exactly his subject. He'd never had a kid. He had no bits of wisdom to impart. He might have tried to ease her mind about her husband becoming a detective, he guessed. Hell, it wasn't his place. That was between Sally and Dave.

"So you found my note?" asked McManaway.

"Yeah. What's it about?"

"I was out by the viaduct this morning and I saw Darrell Phillips puttering around in front of his store. Turns out his wife signed him out of the mental health center after just one day."

"Not surprising, is it? Ask her, and she'll give you the story about her husband having an appointment with a private psychiatrist."

"That's not the thing. Seeing Phillips made me remember

you wanted me to check on his military record when I had a chance. I made a few calls. It wasn't as difficult to get as I feared. I must be getting good at doing your hackwork."

"And?"

"Harter, you won't believe this."

• • •

Tuesday was Darrell Phillips' club night and he'd already left, Vi Phillips told Harter as he followed her up the stairs to the apartment over the appliance dealership. Both she and the apartment gave off a feeling of spotlessness and tidiness. This wasn't an early-morning distress call, and Mrs. Phillips was considerably more composed than the previous times he'd seen her. Her red hair looked like she'd just come from the beauty parlor.

Harter thought twice about sitting on the white couch, not wanting to leave a smudge, but most of the other furniture was white, too, and the tables were all covered with frilly doilies and fragile bric-a-brac, so he supposed the sofa was as good a place to drop as anywhere else. He declined the coffee she offered and waited for her to sit down before he opened up.

As if to cut him off at the pass, she explained that her husband had spent Sunday night at Shawnee Mental Health Center, and on Monday she'd taken Darrell to his own doctor, who saw no reason he couldn't come home. Whatever was troubling him, he wasn't dangerous, she insisted. The last two days he'd been perfectly normal.

"I'm not here to hassle you over signing him out," said Harter. "It's about your husband's military record. Vietnam has come up several times."

"That's not unusual, is it? If we're to believe what we hear, a lot of veterans have difficulty forgetting Vietnam, Detective."

"Usually they've been there."

170

"What?"

"The ones who have trouble forgetting are usually the ones with something to forget."

"You mean Darrell was never in Vietnam?"

"Not unless he went as a tourist, which isn't very likely."

"Then—"

"Then what?"

"There must be some mistake." She was obviously shaken. Her voice had become high and thin.

"I don't think so. We made a number of calls today. We've asked for verification in writing, but, if you know the army, that may take a while. I thought you ought to know sooner."

"This doesn't make any sense."

"No, it doesn't. What did he ever say about his service record?"

"I think I told you he doesn't speak much about it, at least not about the details. Darrell and I have been married for six years. It's the second marriage for both of us. I met him when I came here as office manager for a construction company in 1978. After my divorce, I wanted to get out of my hometown. I imagine I never really felt the need to probe him about the war. Of course, I'd listen if he mentioned something."

"What did he mention?"

She shrugged.

"Do any of his old army buddies come to visit?"

She seemed to think for a second, then answered, "No."

"Apparently he was never in the service."

"I don't know what to say."

"Neither do I. Do you remember him ever bringing up Vietnam with anyone else? Maybe his ex-wife would know."

"She—she doesn't live in Shawnee any longer. As far as others, I just don't know. It wasn't exactly a frequent topic of conversation. I took whatever he said at face value. By the time we married, both of his parents were dead, and I had no reason to doubt anything he said. Actually, I don't believe he mentioned Vietnam until the last couple of years. I was a little surprised myself when it first came up. Mostly he talked in generalities about how terrible it had been."

"But he never talked about it in front of other people?"

"Not that I can recall."

"Did something happen two or three years ago—some bad situation like the flood—something that could have unnerved him?"

"You mean something to start him talking about the war?"

"Yeah."

Again, she seemed to think for a minute, then shook her head no. "Unless it was the recession. That's when our business began to drop off."

"Your marriage wasn't on the rocks, was it? Was either of you seeing someone else?" There, he'd asked it. "He does keep confessing to shooting you, you know."

"Those things are none of your business, but, no, there's nothing like that."

Her voice had become a husky whisper, and he could tell how hurt she was by the question. *Why did he keep bulldozing over good people?* He rubbed his fingers against the soft white fabric of the couch. "You say your husband doesn't have a drug or alcohol problem?"

"No, he doesn't." Her voice was louder. The hurt was turning into anger.

"And he has no gun?"

"No," she said emphatically.

"Would you like me to wait until he comes home and we could take him over to the mental health center again?"

"What I'd truly like is for you to leave, Detective Harter. Darrell isn't violent. He may be mixed up right now, but he'd never hurt anybody. He's been a perfect husband. He's just upset by the flood or something. I'll call his doctor tonight and we'll decide what to do."

"I don't want to feel responsible if anything happens to you."

"Nothing is going to happen to me. Darrell and I will work this out. I wouldn't have him committed to Crimpton State Hospital for anything. And I won't wreck everything we've struggled for."

"Do you think, perhaps, he feels guilty about not going to Vietnam?"

"I think you better leave. Darrell's done nothing." Though her voice was white hot, her eyes were nearly as red as her hair. She was ready to start bawling the minute he left. "Please go, Detective. Darrell and I will solve whatever problems he has."

He stared across the room at her for quite a while. Finally, he stood up. "If that's what you want, Mrs. Phillips."

"It's what I want."

"Call me if anything happens, if it even looks like something might happen," he said.

"What if they're wrong? What if the army made some mistake, simply lost Darrell's files or some such confusion?"

It was Harter's turn to shrug. "I told you, we're expecting a written statement."

Mrs. Phillips just sat in her white chair, watching him edge toward the door, making no move to escort him, holding herself in until he was gone.

Outside, in his car, he couldn't decide if he was doing the right thing by driving away. One part of him wanted to wait there until Darrell Phillips came back from his club meeting, wait there all night if need be. Another part told him there was little or nothing he could do. He couldn't just sit outside the

173

appliance store night after night. What if she was right? What if the army was wrong? Wouldn't be the first time.

He lit a cigarette but barely puffed on it. Just held it between his fingers as it burned down to the filter. The streetlights bounced off the old viaduct across from the store. The night was clear and the moon was fattening toward full belly.

After fifteen or twenty minutes, he turned the key. Maybe Len Schiller was home.

··· 27 ···

The alley was a narrow one-way street, but he wasn't about to have Schiller leave him in the dust again, so he pulled into it the wrong way. He wasn't going to park out on Billings Street and stroll mannerly up to the front door so the goddamn punk could slip out the back another time. If Len Schiller escaped him this time, he'd be hoofing it.

He dodged a world-class collection of potholes at the alley's mouth, and then his headlights were shooting straight up into the headlights of the van parked behind the brick white elephant, the gray van that had speeded away a few hours earlier. Looked like the vehicle's rear doors were swung open, and suddenly a girl came around from the back and stood sentry beside the van. He left his engine running and his lights on. She eyed him as he walked toward her.

At first, she reminded him of the girl he'd noticed that morning at the community college, the one with the black tights and frizzed-up hair. This one, too, wore a slick, shiny jacket, and her hair was mussed like she'd slept on the same side of her head for three nights' running. Drawing closer, he saw there really wasn't much similarity. *Girl* wasn't even the right word for her. She looked to be in her late thirties. Her dour,

175

distrusting expression, combined with the alley shadows and harsh headlights, made her pale face appear even harder, more lined, more tired than it probably did on a good day.

"You'll have to move," she said. "You're blocking us in."

He stepped around her and inspected the rear of the van. It was two-thirds loaded with stereo and TV equipment, cardboard boxes of stuff, clothes, and small furniture. "Schiller let you do all the lifting and hauling?" he asked. "Where is he?"

"You a cop or what?"

"Or what."

"He's inside."

Before he crossed the tiny backyard to the kitchen, Harter side-tripped to his car, turned off the motor and lights, and removed his keys.

The door was wide open and he saw Schiller before Schiller saw him. They hadn't taken away all the kitchen furniture yet, and Roger Wilton's old buddy was sitting at the table, back to the door, busy on the phone. He was decked out in full costume, black jeans and leather jacket, and looked like he'd gained a few pounds since Harter had last seen him.

"We'll be out of here in an hour or two," he said to someone.

"Len—" The woman pushed past Harter and into the kitchen. "Len—"

Schiller turned, saw Harter in the doorway, and cut off the phone talk fast. "What the fuck do you want?"

"Just walking the beat," said Harter. "Saw the van out there and wanted to be sure no one was ripping you off while you were out earning an honest buck. Just protecting upstanding citizens."

"Don't get fucking sarcastic with me, Harter."

"So he is a cop?" asked the woman. "He gave me a smart-

176

ass answer when I asked him. He's got the alley blocked. He seemed to know you."

"He's a cop, all right, and he likes to think he knows me. Likes to think he knows everyone. Makes up shit about people, about them breaking the precious law," Schiller told her.

"We're still leaving here tonight, aren't we?" she asked.

"No sweat, Patty. He's just a fucking sixty-second man. Make another trip through this hole to be sure we ain't leaving nothing, and I'll take care of him."

"She your wife or girlfriend?" asked Harter as soon as Patty was gone.

"None of your business, is it?" said Schiller.

"Same old warm Len."

"You didn't come here to share a beer. I asked you before—what do you want?"

"Actually you asked me what the *fuck* I wanted. Someone should teach you to speak civilly."

"You ain't the one to teach me nothing."

"Can I come in, or do you want me to just stand here in the doorway?"

"Got a search warrant? Got a battalion of pigs out there?"

"Christ, you're a walking museum, aren't you? *Pigs.* Haven't heard that one in years. It's Nineteen eighty-five, you know. You're not a teenager anymore. No, I don't have a search warrant, but I'll get one if you want. And I came by myself. For a chat. Call it deep background. Isn't that what all the politicians and reporters say? I want to know about Roger Wilton."

"Is he the one they found dead out on the mountain the other day?"

"Yeah. I hear you used to know him."

"Maybe. Maybe I knew him. I'm like you, Harter. I know a shitload of people. They come and they go. Haven't seen him

177

since the sixties. Never gave him a thought till I read about him being shot. You sure he was shot? Sure he didn't OD or something?"

"Shot twice in the chest." Harter stepped into the room and, when Schiller didn't protest, crossed to the far end of the table and sat down. "Why do you think he might have overdosed?"

"Just small talk, just keeping up my end of the conversation."

"Was he into drugs when you knew him?"

"Lots of people were into lots of shit in those days. There's stockbrokers and judges who were hippies then. What'd Roger turn out to be?"

"A groundskeeper."

"Figures."

"Looks like he came back to town last Friday. He probably heard about the bones being found at his family's house in Shantytown."

"Seems like I heard that, too. Last week's news, wasn't it? Long time ago, last week."

"Like the sixties."

"Yeah. Like the sixties."

"The bones date to the sixties."

"Lots of skeletons probably do. What's it got to do with me? You accusing me of shooting Wilton, or killing a woman twenty years ago and burying her body behind his house?"

"I'm not accusing you of anything."

"Sure as hell sounds like you are. You ain't even read me my rights."

"For such a goddamn innocent, you're pretty touchy, Schiller."

"I'm tired of you assholes harassing me all the fucking time.

That's one reason Patty and me are leaving. Going to start fresh."

"You sure you're not packing up because you saw me come by this afternoon? I saw the van scoot away. You got a condo waiting for you in Miami?"

"I'm clean, you son of a bitch. Haven't been in no alleged trouble for a long time. Can't a man improve himself? We're just getting out of Shawnee. Got to be out by the fifteenth or pay another month's rent. Patty and me are moving to a farm in West Virginia, a couple hours' south of here. Should have moved to the country ten years ago when the notion first struck me."

"Back to nature, huh?"

"Something wrong with that?"

"Nice pipe dream."

"Don't fucking bait me."

"I just don't picture you as a country boy. You'd be out of your element. Unless you intend to do some farming. Maybe get into the supply end of the business."

"Shit, man. I let you come in here and you sit there and insult me over and over. You want to know about Wilton and wind up accusing me of killing people and dealing drugs. I should call my goddamn lawyer."

"Can't we finish moving shit?" asked Patty from the doorway behind Harter. "Isn't he gone yet?"

"Go back in the other room," Schiller told her.

Harter sat silent for minute, studying the wall above the table, the wall with all the old photos and posters plastered over it. "You don't have a picture of Roger Wilton, do you? Some of these look as old as the sixties."

"Hell, I don't know what you'll find stuck up there. I keep telling you I haven't seen Wilton since—what was it?—'sixty-seven or 'sixty-eight."

"Since he left town after his mother was killed."

"You trying to pin that on me, too?"

"Did you ever meet his mother or any of his family?"

"Maybe. I don't know. Nothing about them sticks with me. Christ, I can't even remember some of my own aunts and uncles."

"They're probably happy about that."

"Stop fucking insulting me!"

"How about any of the girls he hung out with? Maybe a Joyce Dillard or a Christine Malcolm. They called her Christy, and she was the one he'd have been seeing right before he left. She went away to college in California that fall."

"Was she the one with the big tits and tight little moneymaker?"

Harter pictured Joyce Bertoia in the library, dreading attacks of high school memories, and Gerald Malcolm at his desk, still sad about his daughter's death, and it was all he could do to keep from reaching over and grabbing Schiller by his long greasy hair.

Even Schiller must have sensed his anger, for he was more careful when he spoke again. "So, her name was Malcolm, was it? We didn't use last names much, you know. It was Roger and Len and Christy. Never knew much about her. Anything else you want to know? Any more blasts from the past? Look, I need to get out of here."

"I'd prefer you stay around for a while. I may want to talk to you again."

Schiller shook his head. "Told you. Got to be out by the fifteenth. You going to pay next month's rent if we're not?"

"You've got a couple days. You'll be a hell of a lot more comfortable here than in jail. I'm sure I could come up with a reason to hold you for forty-eight hours if I put my mind to it. Your choice."

"Goddamn, Harter. More of your fucking harassment. I don't know nothing about no bones or Roger Wilton's mother or no Malcolm girl."

"And you never saw Roger over the weekend? He didn't call you from the motel Friday night or Saturday after he came back?"

"I never saw the bastard for seventeen years, almost half my life. He never called me from the Goodnight Motel or anywhere else."

"How'd you know that?"

"What?"

"How'd you know Roger stayed at the Goodnight Motel?"

"Read it in the paper."

"No. Even if you could read, it wasn't in the paper. We never released it. All the paper mentioned was finding his car by the high school."

"Look, Harter, it's all over the fucking street, about the motel. There's other ways of finding shit out."

"It's still a good reason to hold you for a while. You want to hear your rights now?"

"Put your hands on the table," ordered Patty.

Harter felt pretty dumb when he looked over his shoulder and saw the pistol in her hand. He'd ignored all the rules, bypassed common sense. Showed up alone, and even tipped off a punk like Schiller that he had. Forgotten that anything could happen. Forgotten about the molemen. And they'd come.

Schiller was moving around the table now, keeping his distance from Harter. When he got beside Patty, she gave him the gun. "He's got his under his jacket," Schiller told her. "Reach under and take it." She seemed a little reluctant.

"You going to dump me on Black's Mountain, too? Going to abandon my car up by East Shawnee High?" taunted Harter.

"Get his gun," Schiller ordered again.

Harter waited for Patty to lean over and reach inside his jacket. He knew he'd only have one chance. One chance to put every muscle in action, to throw her behind him, between Schiller and him, between the gun and his back. If Schiller was fast on the trigger, if Patty was harder to toss than he suspected, if he rammed his knee into the table leg when he twisted around, it was all over.

Patty bent forward slightly and, as she started to slide her hand in for his gun, Harter scraped his chair back like he was giving her more room. Then, in one long motion, he grabbed her by the waist and, rolling to the linoleum, shoved her toward Schiller with all the strength he could manage.

He was pulling out his gun when Schiller's went off, and then Patty was falling heavy on top of him. At first he thought she'd been shot in the mix-up, but then she was screaming and banging her fists against him and he realized Schiller had just thrown her at him like he'd thrown her at Schiller.

He pushed her off of him so rough that he heard her body slam against the cabinet beneath the sink. He pointed his gun at the doorway, but Schiller was gone.

He climbed to his feet and headed cautiously for the living room. The hall door was open and he could hear the punk scrambling up the steps into the huge building's maze of empty rooms.

The steps creaked as Harter followed. Step by step, creak by creak. Up to the third floor. At least it wasn't as dark as he feared. Along the derelict hall, doors were open or missing, allowing in streaks of light from the moon and from the streetlights out front.

The first room was the toughest. He flattened himself against the wall just outside, like they taught you to, and then he jumped in, ready to fire. No one was there.

One by one, room by room, he worked his way down the hall, revolver ready. Never anyone there.

It was a long hall and he was almost convinced Schiller had escaped, had run down the stairs at the far end, when he heard the glass break in a room on the alley side.

He rushed through the doorway in time to see Schiller leap down onto the roof of a lean-to, a shed that abutted the building. The punk hit the tin roof hard and took a while to straighten up. When he did, he spotted Harter in the window and pulled off a shot.

Harter aimed for his gun hand, but then Schiller moved and his chest seemed to explode when the bullet cut into it. There was a long howl and then Schiller fell off the lean-to and thumped against the ground.

Patty was a good driver. She backed the van out of the alley as fast as anyone would have dared to drive it forward. All Harter could do was watch her go.

··· 28 ···

His fingers drummed on the edge of the kitchen table. He kept telling himself how stupid he'd been to have fallen in such a hole.

"She won't get far," said Sergeant Wayne Smith. "Schiller had more than ten thousand dollars on him. He had to have been carrying most of the cash. Probably didn't trust her. She's in that van and she'll have to be stopping for gas. She'll be easy to spot."

"She might be heading into West Virginia," said Harter, staring up at the collage over the table. "Schiller talked about moving."

"Where?" asked the state cop.

"He said a couple hours south of here."

"That takes in a good chunk of the state."

"I know. He may have been lying anyway." Harter reached up and lifted a clipping to see what was underneath it.

"We'll get her and she'll pour it out."

"If she knows much."

"She has to know something. If you're right, if Wilton called Schiller from the motel and Schiller bumped him off for some reason, then she had to help, at least in moving the vehicles around. It all has to have something to do with those god-damn bones. I bet you're right that it was Wilton who wanted to meet you at the train station Saturday night. We know from the tape he could have explained things, and that's probably why he wanted to see you. Schiller just got to him first. Hell, he might have shot Wilton right here. We'll look around upstairs tomorrow morning in the daylight. The van was perfect for hauling the body out to Black's Mountain. It all fits."

"Nothing fits." Harter stood up for a better view of a picture of a group of long-haired kids. "There's no reason. No motive. It's not like the movies where it's boom-boom, the bad guys get blown away, and everything's suddenly crystal clear. We don't know a hell of a lot more than we did a few hours ago."

"We know Schiller and Patty were connected somehow with Wilton's murder," said Dave McManaway, who'd been pretty quiet since showing up. "They wouldn't have pulled a gun on you if they weren't worried. I wish I'd been with you."

Harter shrugged. "It was my fault. I walked in here cocky and blind."

"I'd have done the same," said Smith.

"It's got to be them," said Harter.

"Sure it does."

"No. This photo." He reached up and pulled the old snapshot off the wall. "It's got to be them. I've studied Roger's face enough times to recognize him. He's got his arm around a girl, and it's not Joyce Dillard. I bet it's Christy Malcolm. That's Schiller on the other side of her. Christ, he looks eighteen or nineteen, almost human. Maybe he really had a mother and didn't raise up from a manure pile. What the hell happened in Nineteen sixty-seven? What happened to these people?"

"You're getting punch drunk," said Smith. "Go home and

sleep as long as you want. Headquarters can live without you tomorrow, can't it, McManaway? We'll finish up here."

Harter didn't bother to argue. He went out the door with the picture in his hand.

• • •

—*Night   In the shed   We pushed   We moved everything out of the way and kept dampening the ground so it was easier to dig   So the same thing didn't happen to me   Christ, I can't do this   Can't risk putting this down on tape   Got people to see   Can't use their names   Have to change all the names like Dylan sang in "Desolation Row"   She—*

She what?

She who?

Roger's mother?

The girl they were burying?

All tangled up, these people. The more he stared at the photos he'd collected, the more he listened to the tape from the motel room, the more he ran back over what he'd learned and the people he'd questioned, the more tangled up they got. Mother and son and girlfriends and jerks and old men. Generations swirling in floodwater together. 1940s/1960s/1980s. One thing leads to another. Middle-aged men with habits.

Harter could see Roger Wilton talking into the tape recorder at the Goodnight Motel, could see him struggling with the past, and with the future, with what he would do.

He leaned forward and switched off the cassette player on the coffee table in front of the couch. He reached for his cigarettes, lit one, then glanced again at the pictures, the yearbooks, the reports, the notes, all spread around the table and the rug. He'd spent the morning sifting through it all, and now it was lunchtime. Now it was time to get something in his stomach other than caffeine.

186

He'd slept badly Tuesday night. Kept being surprised by Patty with a gun in her hand. Kept going down a dark corridor, room to room in an old building's innards. Kept seeing Schiller falling from the lean-to roof with a hole in his chest. Hadn't meant to kill him. Kept watching Patty drive off. Kept wondering why nothing fit.

He'd thought about going to Liz's after Wayne Smith had sent him home from Schiller's. Wanted to go to the West Side and have her put her arms around him and not say a damn thing, just wanted to feel her, make sure she was still alive, find some other way to communicate than words. But he hadn't.

He rubbed out his cigarette and found himself staring at Roger Wilton's graduation photo and, from the yearbook page, Roger stared back. Best-Looking Boy, 1966. Devilish, or worse, in his tie. The sort to play graveyard pranks. Dark eyes like his mother's.

Nan Nash, East Shawnee class of 1941, black sweater and pearls, big smile. Most Likely to Succeed. To be a nurse. Nurses and schoolteachers, the paths open to women in those days.

Roger and Nan on the porch of the Egypt Street house on a fifties afternoon, only yards from where a body would be buried years later.

Roger with his hippie friends, 1967, before he'd left town. His arm around a girl. Had to be Christy Malcolm. Who'd gone to San Francisco late in 1967. Who, according to her father, had gone away to escape the Wilton boy, who had also run away to escape something. Or someone. Schiller said Christy had big tits and a tight little moneymaker. He was in the photo, too. Schiller, his eyes on Christy, but she was turned away from him, turned toward Roger.

Harter picked up his magnifying glass and held it over the girl's pretty face. Her lips were parted like she was whispering to Roger. Maybe she was saying, "Let's get away from this asshole Len." Her long dark hair was tucked behind her left ear. There was an earring. Light-colored. Shaped like a semicircle. Like a half-moon.

He looked at the girl and the earring a long time before he put down the magnifying glass, lit another cigarette, and picked up the phone. A woman answered and he figured she was Karen, the pregnant black girl. Once Gerald Malcolm was on the line, he told him about shooting Schiller the night before. It would be in the papers soon enough. Then, he said he was working on his investigation report and needed to tie up a few strands. He wanted the report to be as complete as possible so no one would ever have to go down the same blind alleys he had, he said. What college, he wondered, had Christy moved to San Francisco to attend?

After that, he called Dave McManaway and Pete Epstein and told them what he wanted them to do.

Other people set in motion, he went out the door, down the two flights of steps, and outside to his car. The Wednesday afternoon traffic was light as he drove the Avenue to South Shawnee.

He wasn't exactly sure what he was after, but was working on feelings. He felt like he should visit Shantytown again. The same sort of feeling was what took him up to the overlook time after time. Sometimes he just had to see things again, like looking at old photos, like trying to resurrect the moments trapped in them.

The leavings of the flood were still apparent as he drove along Egypt Street. Only a little more than a week before, the street had been underwater, the shed had floated away, the bones had been exposed, and this had all begun. No matter how fast life seemed to move these days, a week wasn't very long at all.

··· 29 ···

"God spared us," said Spilky. He'd opened his door to let out his cat and seen Harter getting out of his car. Or maybe he'd seen Harter climb out of his car, so he'd opened the door to let the cat out. Anyway, Matt Curry's neighbor had stepped down to the street, asked Harter about the investigation, then launched into his spiel. "Didn't seem possible a week ago, but now everything's returning to normal. We were discussing it at church Sunday. The pastor said God must have plans for us and let us off light this time. In Bible class, a man said maybe the reason for the flood was to uncover those bones so the killer would be punished for his past sins. God works in mysterious ways."

"I've heard that crap before," said Harter, wishing he could have avoided the whole conversation. "You really believe folks upriver lost their homes, and three dozen drowned, so an old score could be settled? Hell, there was a bishop in the Nineteen twenties who proclaimed an earthquake was caused by God's wrath over flappers wearing short skirts. I don't buy any of it. I've got nothing against short skirts. The flood was just chance. Too much rain at the wrong time. You weren't the instrument of God because you and your wife happened to be the ones who came along first. That was chance, too."

189

"There has to be some meaning," Spilky insisted.

"No, there doesn't," said Harter, turning away.

As he headed down the bank to the Wilton house, he worried he shouldn't have opened his mouth. All he needed was a call to the chief complaining about his irreverence. The powers-that-be were always sensitive as hell whenever God got dragged into it, so usually he kept his opinions to himself when dealing with the public. Usually he penned in all thoughts about politics and religion, those deadly subjects. Usually he let the fools have the podium and walked away. But Spilky had caught him off guard. Like so much had recently. Like Patty and Len Schiller had.

He'd better do a repair job on his guard. The damn thing kept falling off.

• • •

From his front window, Matt Curry watched Harter go around the side of the Wilton place. The cop seemed distracted. Had Spilky said something important to him? Harter stopped near the roped-off hole where the shed had been and just stood there, staring into the hole for a long time. Not budging. Frozen in place like the ancient threesome in his memory of the old farmhouse at the edge of town. Waiting for the rocks to fall.

Curry had stood by the hole himself two nights before, after learning about Roger's death, after talking to Flathead about what Harter had asked him. He'd tried to sleep, but couldn't. Tried to read Mark Twain until his eyes fell shut, but they didn't. Kept picking up the earring he'd found in the shed shortly after Nan had been run down. Kept going over what he knew, and what he didn't, and telling himself he ought to call Harter, then deciding not to.

He'd crossed Egypt Street in the middle of the night and

190

shined a flashlight down into the grave, as if there was something to see, something he'd missed all along, something that
added up to sense, but the only thing that kept coming to him
was that he didn't want to hurt her. He and Flathead had
pledged themselves not to damage her. He'd never do anything
to hurt her.

But . . .

But the bones had been found after all these years, and
Roger was dead, and the detective kept returning to Shantytown, kept staring into the hole, kept asking questions.

Something he'd told Harter nagged at him. He'd put Nan
in a bad light and he shouldn't have. He didn't know why he'd
done it, except that once the story started to come out, he'd
found himself cutting back on the details to cover up. He'd even
said Wheat had been the one who'd told him, but really it had
been Nan. She'd come to his house that night with a purple
bruise beneath her eye and confessed she'd been ready to kill
Wheat.

Wheat had hit her. He'd accused her of being unfaithful,
and he'd hit her. Wheat didn't know who her lover was—at
least, that's what Nan had said—but he could feel in his bones
that his wife had a lover.

Lover. She came over to him, her arms reaching out, and his
to hers. He pulled her down on top of him and rubbed at her
smooth back, down to her buttocks. So soft against his hard.
Touching him down there where no one else ever had. And
then, sliding into her so easy. Never anyone else but her.
Wrapped in her warm wet, like he was born to be there, like
nothing mattered more than those moments. *Lovers.*

Wheat had hit her. Then, after supper the next evening,
he'd started in again. Yelling, accusing. She was washing the
dishes and she had this knife in her hand and she turned and
threw it. She hadn't meant to kill him. Nan never would have

hurt anyone intentionally. If she'd really wanted to, she'd have got him with the knife, but she didn't. She'd never kill anyone. Curry believed that. He wished there was a way to get the point across to Harter without having to bring up all sorts of other questions.

Harter just stood by the hole, like the earth was telling him something. Not far from the cop, another spectator had staked out a position. The Spilkys' cat had wandered across the street and seemed to be watching the detective watch the grave. It wasn't a bad-luck black cat, rather an orangish mixed breed, and Curry liked it better than he liked his neighbors. After a while, the cat rose from its sprawl and prowled around a little, moving with that shoulder strut cats have. The creature circled a spot a couple times. Then, after it had done its business, it began pawing at the ground, shoveling soft, muddy soil over its waste, like it didn't want anyone to know what it had done.

A pickup truck with a camper top came down Egypt Street and parked in front of his house. Curry didn't recognize Bill Merrill at first. He didn't know when he'd last seen Wheat's son-in-law, but, as the big man made his way toward Harter, he decided that was who it was. Nan had never liked Bill Merrill. No, that wasn't it. It wasn't so much that she didn't like him as that she hadn't wanted Dorothy to marry so young. She'd hoped the girl would finish school and become the nurse she never was, the one her mother had wanted her to be. She'd had huge hopes for Roger, too.

Why didn't things ever work out?

Lovers.

● ● ●

As Harter walked to the front of the house to meet Bill Merrill, he noticed the expression on Merrill's face tighten in surprise. He obviously hadn't expected to run into the detective.

192

"Day off?" Harter asked.

"I finagled the afternoon," said Merrill. "Truth is, I haven't been here since the flood. I've been working, and I kept putting it off. Didn't want to face it. Besides, after the news about the woman buried here, Dorothy and I thought it might be best to stay away a few days. Is that the place?"

Harter nodded. "Nothing there but a hole now."

"My son and a friend of his are coming down after school. We won't be getting in your way by going inside, will we?" asked Merrill. "We wanted to check the house out and decide what to do with it. My vote's to just tear it down, but it's not my homeplace. I'm not sentimental about the damn thing like Dorothy and Wheat. To me, it's an albatross. Sure as hell won't sell now."

"I don't care what you do," said Harter. "Just let me know if you find more bones."

Merrill gave him a strange stare. "I hope we don't find more bones. Are you expecting more?"

Harter shrugged. "How are Wheat and Dorothy these days?"

"About the same as on Sunday. Dorothy's a little depressed. First the skeleton, then her brother's murder. She worries what our friends are thinking. Wheat may be a little worse than a week ago. I don't know how much he understands about the flood and the bones, but he seems to be deteriorating. Could be he's just another week older. We never bothered to explain to him about Roger. Didn't see much reason."

"You didn't like Roger, did you?"

"Told you as much the other day, didn't I?"

"Guess you did. You know, I'm looking into his friends from the sixties. Did you ever hear of a guy named Len Schiller?"

Merrill shook his head without saying anything. Harter

found it odd he didn't have more curiosity. Merrill didn't appear at all concerned what might have happened to his brother-in-law, so Harter didn't offer anything about Tuesday night at Schiller's. The shooting had been too late for the morning paper, and apparently not many people knew about it yet.

"How about a girl named Christy Malcolm?" he asked. "Roger seems to have seen a lot of her in Nineteen sixty-six and 'sixty-seven."

"Keep telling you, I didn't keep up with him," said Merrill. "Had no use for him. But *Malcolm* . . . the name sounds familiar somehow."

Harter remembered sitting in the Merrills' kitchen on Thursday, and a remark from Dorothy about her husband's school days. "Maybe you know the name from church. Christy Malcolm would have gone to the same Catholic school you did, though she'd have been there several years later. Her father, Gerald Malcolm, used to be a math teacher at East Shawnee High."

"Maybe that's it, then. I could know the family from church, not that I go much anymore. The name just stuck. Can't really tell you much about them. What's the Malcolm girl got to do with Roger's killing, anyway?"

"We don't know."

"Well, whatever you know is probably more than I do. I just married into the Wilton clan, you understand. They aren't exactly my people. I never really got along with Nan, and I couldn't tolerate Roger and his hippie ways. When they all lived here, I visited this house as little as possible. It's a pain to have to deal with it now. Wheat's all right, as far as I'm concerned, but Nan was something else. Over the years, I've grown to like Wheat, and you must have noticed that Dorothy's absolutely devoted to him. Wheat never gave me trouble like Nan did."

"Your wife seems to have mixed feelings about her mother, too. Why?"

"We went over this the other day, didn't we? I don't see how it's any of your business, Detective."

How many times had Harter heard that line? How many times in the last week had he answered that he wasn't sure what was his business and what wasn't? How many times had he simply plowed ahead? Here he was again. *Bulldozing over good people.*

"What was wrong between your wife and her mother?"

Bill Merrill avoided an answer as long as he could, but finally he must have realized Harter would stand at his elbow the rest of the day if he didn't open up. "Nan didn't want Dorothy and me to get married," he said. "She tried everything she could think of to stop us."

Bulldozing again. "Why?" The big uncomfortable question.

"I was out of school when we started going together, but Dorothy wasn't. Nan wanted her to graduate and go on to college, but Dorothy got pregnant. We don't really talk about it, but it was no secret. I don't know what it's like these days, but twenty-five years ago they didn't want pregnant girls to attend classes at the high school. I don't know whether there was a law against it, but they certainly discouraged it. They called Dorothy down to talk to the guidance counselor and principal. They didn't want the other girls tainted, I guess, as if none of the others ever spread their legs. You can see it still makes me mad. Anyway, Dorothy would have had to quit school, and Nan didn't want her to. My folks were real religious and they were pressuring me to marry her, but Nan wouldn't give her consent. Finally, Wheat did."

"And Nan never gave in?"

"No. She was bullheaded as hell. You had to know her to understand. She kept telling Dorothy that marrying me would wreck her life, that she was too young to be *trapped* like that. One night Nan told her that she'd been pregnant when she'd married Wheat and she'd always regretted it. It was a crummy thing to unload on your daughter, especially since it was Dorothy who Nan had been carrying. She insinuated she'd had an unhappy life and wished she'd never married Wheat. Dorothy still cries when she talks about it. Here was her own mother telling her she wished she'd never married her father."

"Must have been tough," sympathized Harter. "Back then, there was certainly a lot of stigma attached to an unmarried girl having a baby. Your wife was caught in a real bind."

"Oh, Nan didn't want her to have the baby."

"She didn't?"

"She offered Dorothy an abortion."

"An abortion? They were illegal then."

"Yeah. A woman couldn't just stroll into some clinic, have it done, and stroll out again the same day. It was all back-alley stuff. Nan claimed she knew how to do it. Dorothy's grandmother had been a midwife, and growing up, Nan had picked up a lot about childbearing and all sorts of old wives' tales about how to end a pregnancy. She had books, too."

"Her brother told me she'd wanted to be a nurse," said Harter.

Merrill nodded, silent as if he'd said too much.

"Dorothy refused the abortion, and you two got married?"

"Right. And Nan was wrong. Dorothy and I are still together. She'd kill me if she found out I told you all this."

"Do you know if Nan Wilton ever performed abortions for other women?"

"I have no idea."

Harter glanced across Egypt Street at Matt Curry's house. In his mind, a whole new set of questions for the old man was forming.

··· 30 ···

Hard to line all the ducks in a row   Didn't know what to do that night either   Nineteen sixty-seven   Mom   In the shed   Lucky the old man was away   They'd called him out to a train wreck in the country someplace and he was gone every night that week   We knew we had to do it then   The old bastard never would have understood   He'd have climbed on his high horse   Mom said it wasn't good but it was right   She promised to help so   it didn't happen to me what—(roar of a truck)—Night   In the shed   We pushed   We moved everything out of the way and kept dampening the ground so it was easier to dig   So the same thing didn't happen to me   Christ, I can't do this   Can't risk putting this down on tape   Got people to see   Can't use their names   Have to change all the names like Dylan sang in "Desolation Row"   She—(click)

"Dylan. My daughter had all of his records," said Pete Epstein. "He was like a god to the kids twenty years ago. First it was Elvis, then the Beatles, then Bob Dylan. I wonder who their gods are today?"

"Bruce Springsteen, Madonna, Michael Jackson, I don't know," said Dave McManaway.

Epstein bent forward and leaned his elbows on his autopsy table, the table where Roger Wilton's body had been stretched out a few days before, the table where the girl's bones had been arranged the last time Harter had been in the medical examiner's office. "Sounds to me like you've figured it out right. It all makes some sort of sense. From what Merrill told you yesterday, even the tape adds up. What was it Wilton said? His mother insisted what they were doing wasn't *good* but it was *right*."

"She didn't want the same thing to happen to him that happened to her," added Harter. "She didn't want it to happen to Dorothy, either. Nan Wilton must have felt awful trapped and frustrated."

"A hell of a lot of women wouldn't choose to go back to the sixties or before," said Epstein. "When people talk of the good old days, they forget what they were really like. I imagine Nan Wilton's feelings about her life weren't so singular."

Harter reached in his pocket for a cigarette. He'd no sooner put the filter between his lips and struck a match than Epstein was saying, "Wish you wouldn't do that in here. I'm a doctor, you know. I'm supposed to warn people against smoking."

"Some people drink," said Harter, but he blew out the match, stuck the cigarette back in his pocket, and mentally scrawled Pete Epstein's name right below Liz's on the list of those trying to save him from himself. "There's no doubt the teeth match?"

"No question. It was a lucky break to find the right dentist so fast. Could have taken days or weeks."

"Glad we finally got one lucky break," said Harter.

"Sad, isn't it? She wouldn't have died today. Roger Wilton would probably be alive, too. Both of their lives would have turned out differently."

"There's nothing about the skeleton that would confirm or deny the girl was pregnant?"

"No. Most likely, she was only a few months along."

"I still don't get what Len Schiller had to do with it," said

198

McManaway, who'd seemed ill at ease all day. Harter wondered if the expectant father was upset by the idea that Nan Wilton had been more than willing to abort a fetus if it kept her daughter from, in Nan's opinion, wrecking her life. To keep *both* of her kids from wrecking their lives, apparently. She must have really regretted marrying Wheat.

"These things happened. Don't let it play tricks on you. Don't let it, for instance, set you against midwives," said Epstein, spinning off in a new direction. "I'm not one of those who want to lock the medical profession's door too tightly. There's a use for midwives. With what hospitals cost today, there's a use for all kinds of alternatives. Hell, hundreds of doctors did the same thing back when abortions were illegal. I knew a few, and they weren't criminals. They simply said yes when some poor girl showed up at their door one night. Seems to me that was better than just letting the baby die after it was born. That happened, too. You've heard the stories. A little old lady passes away, the pillar of her church, and then a baby's remains are found in a trunk in her attic. This time, it was the mother who died. Nan Wilton might have believed she knew what to do, but she obviously didn't." He glanced across the autopsy table at McManaway. "It's damn hard to be as heated up for the right to abortion as the Right-to-Lifers are against it, but . . . God, I sound like a liberal. Save me. Shut me up or I never will be able to get into politics. It's 1985. How many states did Reagan win last year?"

"I promised to vote for you, Pete," said Harter. "You'd be great cutting ribbons at museum openings." He looked over at McManaway. "Ready?"

• • •

Outside, Mother Nature had put on her makeup and was disguising herself as a sexy young dazzler rather than a stormy withered bitch. Her bumps were covered up so her complexion appeared smooth and clear from a distance. Her bright lipstick made the sun feel warm and inviting for a November afternoon. It was like she wanted to seduce you one last time before winter.

They pulled out of Pete Epstein's parking lot, headed down the hill past the Episcopal Church, drove through the downtown, then over the tracks and into the East End, past rowhouses, and north out of town, neither of them saying much. Harter wondered if McManaway's mind was on Sally, ready to give birth to their first child at any moment. But his was with an old man.

After he'd left Bill Merrill the day before, he'd gone across the street to Matt Curry's. It had taken a while, but the retired railroader finally started talking. *And talking*. Harter wasn't sure what had forced open the rusted floodgates, but he sensed Curry had simply been waiting. Waiting a long time to tell someone some things. He wanted Harter to know that, say what you would about her, Nan wasn't evil. Curry would never put up with evil. He loved her.

They turned off the Old Pennsylvania Pike and into the lane that led back to the farmhouse. Connie Malcolm's station wagon was gone again. Perhaps she was on another errand of mercy, as she had been two days earlier. They parked beside Gerald Malcolm's green pickup and slowly got out of their car.

"I'm not looking forward to this," said McManaway as they walked to the porch.

"Neither am I," said Harter.

··· 31 ···

"Me, again." Harter tried to sound as friendly as he could when Karen cracked open the front door. "Is Mr. Malcolm in?"

The pregnant black girl pulled the door open wider and let them step inside. She'd led them halfway down the hall before Gerald Malcolm emerged from his office. "I thought I heard someone ring the bell. Guess I was too deep in farm accounts for it to really register."

"I wasn't sure I should bring them back," said Karen nervously.

"No, it's fine. You can get back to whatever you were doing, Karen." As the girl turned away, Malcolm looked at Harter. "What's on your mind today?"

"A few more questions. Told you yesterday that I'm trying to tie up loose ends so they stay tied. By the way, this is Dave McManaway. He's been assisting me on this case."

"You may not remember, but I sat in your classroom for two years," McManaway said to Malcolm.

"I'm afraid I don't remember. That's not unusual. After a few years, all those student faces seem to blend together. Sometimes it seems half of Shawnee must have sat in my classroom. I hope a few people learned some algebra. Good to see you again, anyway."

Malcolm's tone wasn't very convincing that he was really glad to see McManaway again. Not any more than it was "good" to see Harter another time. Not any more than Harter was really happy about being led into Malcolm's office again.

The room looked much as it had on Tuesday afternoon. Assorted papers still cluttered Gerald Malcolm's desk, but there was no unfinished poster on his wife's. The poster was probably on display in some store window, plugging the benefit for the Allegheny Unwed Mothers Home, guessed Harter.

Malcolm motioned for them to be seated, then leaned his elbow on the edge of his rolltop desk. When neither Harter nor McManaway piped up fast with a question, he said, "I thought you told me on the phone yesterday that your investigation was winding down. You mentioned this fellow Schiller. I read about the shooting in this morning's paper. He sounds like an unsavory sort."

"He was," said Harter.

"And he was the one who murdered Roger Wilton?"

"We believe so. We just don't know why."

"I certainly can't help you on that account, Detective. *The News* seemed to suggest Schiller was heavy in the drug trade. Could it have had something to do with that? Or maybe he and Wilton argued over something that happened when they were young."

"Roger left Shawnee in 'sixty-eight. Seventeen years is a long time to keep a grudge so alive you'd be willing to kill someone over it." Harter reached in his pocket and pulled out a photo. "We found this picture at Schiller's and wanted to know if you recognize anyone in it. Len Schiller's the one on the far right, next to the girl. Roger Wilton's on the other side of her, with his arm around her. I wondered if the girl was Christy, and whether you could identify any of the others. Looks like it might have been taken in Nineteen sixty-seven."

Malcolm half-rose from his chair and leaned forward to reach for the photograph. His slow, deliberate movement reminded Harter that he was dealing with an older man, not a tough punk like Schiller.

Malcolm peered through his thick lenses at the snapshot for a full minute before saying, "Yes, that's Christy. If you hadn't told me it was the Wilton boy, I might not have known him, and I certainly can't put names to any of the rest of them. I didn't approve of the crowd my daughter was running with in those days, Detective. That's why Connie and I encouraged her to go all the way to San Francisco to attend college. We hoped she'd start again and find new friends. But I explained all that to you Tuesday, didn't I?"

"Your daughter was a pretty girl. I studied the picture a long time, too, and I noticed her earring." Harter reached in his jacket pocket again. "It was a lot like these."

Malcolm squinted across the office at the ivory half-moons in Harter's hand, then glanced down again at the photo. "I'm afraid I can't tell if they're similar. I'll take your word for it, if it matters."

"I think it matters, Mr. Malcolm. One of these was found last week at the Wilton house in Shantytown, in the hole where the skeleton was. The other was given to me yesterday by a neighbor who'd picked it up near the same spot in December of 'sixty-seven."

Malcolm reached forward again and handed the picture back to Harter. He suddenly appeared even older than he had a few minutes earlier. He almost seemed to creak, like the steps in the old building on Billings Street where Schiller had lived.

"A couple other things have also turned up, and they don't make sense," said Harter. "We learned your daughter's dental records match the teeth of the skeleton. And, after calling you yesterday, I asked McManaway to check Christy's college records. He learned she was accepted for admission, but never actually registered. She never took a class there. Couldn't have graduated. We couldn't find any verification that she died in San Francisco in Nineteen seventy-eight, either."

"It was Nineteen seventy-seven," said Malcolm.

"Two days ago, you told me it was March Nineteen seventy-eight, just before her twenty-ninth birthday."

"One of us must have been confused. Perhaps it was me. I must have misspoken. Connie and I don't talk about Christy much. It's painful, even now."

"I imagine it is," said Harter. "I'm sorry to keep bringing it up. We'll check on Nineteen seventy-seven, if you like."

Malcolm tilted his head down so his eyes shot at the rug. "You don't have to, Ed."

"You can stop talking to us at any time," said Dave McManaway. "You have rights."

"You have to understand—I didn't kill anyone."

"You have the right to—"

"I didn't kill anyone!"

"So, what happened?" asked Harter, waving off McManaway.

His eyes still on the floor, Malcolm said, "It *was* Christy who was buried by the Wilton house. Doesn't do much good to claim otherwise, does it? She didn't die in Nineteen seventy-eight. Connie and I invented the story about the brain tumor because we just couldn't continue pretending Christy was doing well on the West Coast. Everyone was always inquiring about her. They wondered why she never came home for a visit."

"How did your daughter really die?"

"An abortion that went wrong."

"Performed by Nan Wilton in December Nineteen sixty-seven?"

Malcolm lifted his head and stared across the room at Harter. "You knew all along? Is that why you came here in the first place?"

"I had no idea until yesterday."

"Christy should never have gotten involved with the boy. He was a bad one."

"I don't know," said Harter. "I'm not going to sit in judgment on how bad Roger Wilton was twenty years ago."

"God, the awful things that happened to kids in the sixties," said Malcolm, his voice low and sad. "I saw my students change, and I saw my daughter change. They seemed to change overnight. It was like the world turned upside down and all standards and morality fell off into space. Christy wasn't like that before."

Wasn't like that before. Harter remembered what Mr. Adams, principal of East Shawnee High, had said: *Before the turmoil.*

"Did you know your daughter was planning to get an abortion?"

"Lord, no. We didn't even know she was pregnant. I wish we had, but Christy told us nothing. She was probably afraid of how we'd react. We didn't bring her up like that. She wasn't a bad girl."

"I'm sure she wasn't," said Harter, but something Joyce Dillard Bertoia had said returned to him, too. *Christy was willing to do anything to please Roger,* and Joyce Dillard wasn't. "The people who knew her well say Nan Wilton wasn't such a bad person either. She just wanted her son to finish college. She didn't want him to marry your daughter any more than you wanted Christy to marry him. It's a shame the two of you couldn't have gotten together. Did you ever meet her?"

"No."

Harter considered telling Malcolm more about Nan and the Wiltons. How she had hopes for her son just as he had hopes for his daughter. How everything in her life kept falling apart. First she got knocked up, as her brother Flathead had put it. Then her daughter did, though Bill Merrill had made him promise not to discuss it. Finally, her son got a girl in trouble. He didn't know what they called it now, but that was what they'd called it then. *Got a girl in trouble.* It happened to one after another of the Wiltons, like there was something in their blood that made it inevitable, that pushed them that way. Almost unbelievable—except it had happened. He decided not to go into it all. Malcolm would only use it to justify why Christy should never have gotten involved with Roger and his family. It was too late to explain things away. Years too late.

"When did you learn your daughter was dead?" Harter asked.

"It must have been two days later."

"You didn't know where she was for two days?"

Malcolm looked like the question had dazed him a little. "It wasn't like that at all. We thought she was spending the night with a friend—a girlfriend—so we weren't worried at first. When she wasn't home by the next evening, Connie called to check up on her and we were told she'd only visited the afternoon before for an hour or so. Then I called Roger Wilton, and he said he hadn't seen Christy for several days. He said they'd broken up. I felt like he was lying, and, of course, now I know he was. I told him I was going to contact the police and report her missing."

"And you did?"

"Yes. I called as soon as I got off the phone with him. They were no help. Whoever it was asked me how old she was, and when I told him, he said, 'Well, she's of age.' Then he asked how long she'd been gone, and when I said since the night before, he said to give her a little more time. He suggested she might have run away, as a lot of young people did in the sixties. He wanted to know if I had any reason to believe harm had come to her, and of course I didn't. He told me to call back in a few days if she was still missing."

Harter nodded. Over the years, he'd given the same response to more than one missing-persons report himself. Usually the person turned up and that was as far as it went. "You never called back?"

"No."

"Why?" asked McManaway.

"Early the next morning we got a call from a woman who said Christy had died from an abortion. She said the body was buried where no one would find it."

"Any idea who the woman was?"

"She wouldn't identify herself, but I imagine it was Roger's mother. I'd never have recognized her voice. At first, Connie and I wondered if it was a cruel prank, and we kept waiting for Christy to get in touch."

"I can't believe you didn't tell the police." McManaway sounded almost angry.

"Tell them what? That a mysterious caller claimed my daughter had died from an illegal abortion? We decided to wait and see what happened. I can't explain it. Why do people do what they do sometimes? The longer we kept it quiet, the harder it was to tell anyone. You understand we really weren't certain what had happened."

"So, you eventually concocted the story about her going to San Francisco?" asked Harter.

"Everyone knew she'd be going out there in a few weeks anyway. I suppose she wanted to have the abortion before she left."

"Then you did believe she died from an abortion?"

"Yes. I guess we did. For a while, we feared the body would turn up in an alley someplace, but the days became years and nothing happened. Not until the flood, at least. We did believe it had something to do with Roger, though we didn't know about his mother at the time. If Roger had come to the house that winter, I'd have killed him. I'm not proud of it, but I would have."

"But you didn't kill him Saturday?"

"No. Believe me. It must have been Schiller. He . . ."

"He what?"

"He showed up at the door Saturday afternoon, a few hours after Roger left. Karen answered, just as she did with you, and she was frightened by him. She made him stand outside while she came to get me."

"You say Schiller was here after Roger left. So he visited you, too?"

Malcolm ran his hand back over his bald head and began rubbing at the base of his neck. "Roger Wilton came back to Shawnee after he heard about the body. Of course, he knew it was Christy's, and, of course, Connie and I suspected it was, too. We hadn't talked to him since I called him to question him about Christy all those years ago. We'd read about his mother being killed in an accident, but until he came here Saturday, we didn't really know she was the one who performed the abortion."

"Roger told you everything Saturday?"

Malcolm's head bobbed. "He didn't want anyone to think he or his mother had committed a murder. That's why he came back. He wanted to arrange a meeting with the police so he could tell them the truth. Then he intended to slip out of town and get lost again. I argued that the truth couldn't do anyone any good, but he kept insisting he and his mother never meant to hurt

Christy. Christy wanted the abortion, he said. He wanted to get it off his conscience."

Get it off his conscience. Everyone seemed to want to paint Roger so black that he had no conscience, but he obviously had. He'd never been able to escape the memory of his girl-friend's death in 1967. And he might have been spoiled, but he cared enough about his mother to carry around·that snapshot of the two of them on the Egypt Street porch.

"Roger made an appointment to meet me Saturday night, but he didn't keep it," said Harter. "Schiller had apparently shot him by then. His body was probably on its way to Black's Mountain. Was that the plan you and Schiller came up with?"

Malcolm's lips tightened. "There was no plan exactly. I didn't mean for him to kill Roger. I didn't know he was going to do it. Schiller just seemed to know so much. He acted as if he'd known it all in Nineteen sixty-seven, too, as if Roger might have filled him in before he ran away. Schiller said he'd also heard from Roger that morning and he knew Roger intended to tell everything to the police. He said he was sure my wife and I didn't want the whole world to know what happened to Christy, and he promised to keep it from happening."

"By murdering Roger Wilton?"

"No. He was going to buy Roger off. He said Roger didn't have anything, so it wouldn't take much to keep his mouth shut."

"This doesn't sound like the Len Schiller I knew," said Harter. "What was in it for him?"

"Some money."

"How much?"

"Two thousand dollars. He wanted seven, and said he was going to offer five thousand to Roger to go away. He promised I'd never hear from him again. I guess I felt he was sleazy, but I didn't realize he was such a criminal. At first, I didn't want any part of what he was suggesting, but he was very convincing. Like I said, he knew all the details and seemed to be very familiar with Roger. I kept thinking about the alternatives, about the truth coming out, and finally I gave in. If he could get Roger to keep quiet and go away, it was worth seven thousand dollars to me."

"People have been killed for less," said Harter.

"You have to believe me. I didn't know Schiller would murder him. I'd never have gone along with any of it if I'd had an inkling," pleaded Malcolm. "Roger had disappeared before, and I thought he might be willing to again. I didn't kill anyone. I've never killed anybody in my life."

"Did you pay Schiller on the spot?" asked Harter, remembering the large amount of cash on Schiller's body.

"I don't keep that kind of cash around. I gave him a check."

"Didn't it occur to you that a canceled check might tie you to the murder?"

"I told you—I didn't know there was going to be a murder. Believe me. Schiller said the banks were closed for the weekend, so I had until Monday afternoon to stop payment. Meanwhile, he had the rest of Saturday and Sunday to talk Roger into leaving. He promised I'd get a call one way or another."

"Did you?"

Malcolm nodded. "I'd expected to hear from Roger, but Schiller called me Sunday and said he'd left town. Then Monday morning I read that Roger was dead."

"Why didn't you call the police?"

Malcolm said nothing.

"I take it you made no attempt to stop the check," said Harter. "Schiller kept his half of the bargain, didn't he? Roger was out of the way, and he never got a chance to talk to me. I can't get rid of the feeling that the blood's on your hands, Mr. Malcolm. Did your wife go along with this conspiracy?"

"My God, no. Connie knows nothing about it, not even

210

now. She was away when both Roger and Schiller came to the house. Perhaps, if she'd been here, she'd have talked me out of it. Look, I even wrote the check on the farm account so she'd never see it."

"But she went along with the cover-up story all these years."

"How many times do I have to tell you? I never intended anyone would die."

"Not Nan Wilton, either?"

"Are you suggesting I had something to do with her death?"

"She was hit by a truck in Nineteen sixty-seven, only a day or so after the botched abortion. You're saying you know nothing about it?"

"I don't." Malcolm's voice was becoming a whine. "If I didn't kill the boy in Nineteen sixty-seven, why would I have killed his mother?"

"I have no way of knowing when you're telling the truth and when you're not. You didn't call the police and tell them about your daughter eighteen years ago. You concocted a lie and held to it all this time. You didn't tell me about Roger and Schiller visiting you when I was here Tuesday."

"Who'd want everyone to know their daughter died like Christy did? The truth doesn't really matter after all these years, does it? It can only destroy people. I was a teacher, and Connie has always been active in the church. We've always tried to do good. Why do you think we take in girls like Karen? We've tried to pay our penance."

Harter shook his head in disgust. "Looks like a big bill to me. I hope you've got enough time left to get out of debt."

"We're not the reason our daughter died, Detective. And you're the one who shot the man who murdered Roger Wilton. The full truth couldn't have helped anyone. Not us, not the Wilton family. Who cared?"

"Roger did," said Harter. "Roger Wilton obviously did."

211

··· 32 ···

"*I shot her.*"

Friday morning. Early. For the third time, Harter sat across the interrogation table from Darrell Phillips and listened to Phillips confess. Both of them had Styrofoam cups of coffee in front of them.

As he watched the appliance dealer, Harter considered asking about his war record. Considered opening up the touchy subject of whether Phillips had actually been in Vietnam and what terrors he'd seen there, or whether it had all been just a story, whether Phillips was so deluded he believed he'd been in a war that he hadn't.

But Harter didn't ask. Said nothing. He was no shrink. And he was worn out. Floods and bones. Molemen and bulldozers. Abortions and murders. Mind games and tapes of disembodied voices. Worn out. He decided he'd wait for Dave McManaway and Vi Phillips to show. He'd see what they had to say, what *she* had to say. See if she had any doubts yet about her husband's sanity. See if she was ready yet to sign him into Shawnee Mental Health Center for more than twenty-four hours. For long enough that someone with proper training might figure out what to do with him.

Somehow he felt Vi Phillips would never be ready. He pictured her Tuesday night—before he'd left her white apartment and gone to Schiller's bloody one—pictured her insisting that he leave, that he leave her and her husband alone to solve their problems. Over and over, so many pictures from the past ten days—the past forty years, for that matter—kept reappearing to him. Pictures and words.

Vi Phillips was never going to be ready. But he was. Ready to do whatever legal junk had to be done to stop Phillips from strolling in and confessing another morning. Ready to put an end to it. There had to be an end to it some time.

But it was up to the prosecuting attorney as well. And that was no sure bet. He and McManaway hadn't had any luck when they'd gone to the prosecutor's office Thursday evening after leaving Gerald Malcolm's house. The attorney had patiently heard them out, but in the end he'd announced it would be tough to convince a jury to punish the retired schoolteacher. Malcolm was respected. The death of his daughter would cause sympathy in as many people as would be outraged by the cover-up. There was no one to testify that Malcolm wasn't telling the truth when he said he didn't realize Schiller would murder Roger Wilton. The prosecuting attorney didn't like flimsy cases and he didn't like mistrials and hung juries. He didn't like to lose. He didn't like bad press.

Harter pulled out his cigarettes, lit one, asked Phillips, "You want a smoke?"

Phillips' head was buried in his puffy hands, but it seemed to sway no.

The small interrogation room filled fast with smoke and, for some reason, Harter thought about how much Liz would hate it, would hate the way he worked. No matter what he did, he always seemed to end up irritating her, getting on her nerves. The small things, they added up, and each one added

213

an inch until the distance between them was measured in yards, more yards than he could long-jump, even with a running start. Why they couldn't move toward each other, he couldn't understand. There was lots he didn't understand. He had a feeling he never would.

When the knock hit the door, he hurried out to the hall to hear what Vi Phillips had to say this morning, but the redhead wasn't there.

McManaway looked pale and shaky. Finally he got his lips going. "She's dead," he said. "He shot her."

• • •

A young, uniformed cop was standing guard when Harter and McManaway showed up at the apartment over the appliance store half an hour later. McManaway had posted the cop at the door when, confused, he'd gone down to headquarters to tell Harter in person. At least he hadn't left the crime scene unattended, Harter thought.

Upstairs, the television set still blared in the living room, just as McManaway said he'd found it when he'd first walked in. In the middle of the carpet lay the pistol that Vi Phillips had claimed her husband hadn't owned. Her husband, by now, was in a cell, and the prosecuting attorney and mental health center had been notified, for whatever good they were.

McManaway was still upset. He kept repeating the story of how he'd found her sprawled on the double bed in her blood-soaked nightgown. "I never believed he'd really do it," he said.

"Anything can happen," Harter mumbled.

"You mean you actually thought he'd shoot her?"

"They're all wounded and they live lies."

"Phillips?"

214

"Phillips. The Malcolms. The Wilton family, too. I mean all of them."

"What can we do about it?"

"Not a goddamned thing that I know of. Just wait for the next flood and see what it turns up. See who else's troubles surface. Hell, don't pay any attention to me. I'm tired."

"So am I," said the younger detective.

When the phone rang, neither of them reached for it immediately. Finally, McManaway, either because he couldn't stand the nagging noise or didn't want the beat cop to come upstairs, walked over to the end table and picked up the receiver. The conversation was brief, and after he'd hung up, he said "Damn" and started for the door.

"What's the matter?" Harter asked.

"It's Sally. Her mother's taken her to the hospital. She's in labor. God, I didn't want it to be like this. I thought we had a couple more days. I wanted to be there, Harter. I wanted to drive her up to the hospital myself and stay with her every minute. Doesn't anything ever work out?"

··· 33 ···

A row of frankfurter buns stretched up Al's arm, and Harter watched him slop mustard on the weiners. The crowd was thicker than usual for a Friday afternoon, and it was all Al could do to keep up with the orders.

As they'd walked from headquarters to the restaurant, Harter had poured out the Darrell Phillips saga to Wayne Smith. The tale was new to the state cop and he seemed to accept that Harter's sadness and frustration were multiplied by the other events of the last week and a half.

Inside Al's, Harter had staked out a seat in the rear corner, his back to the wall, his eyes facing the hot dog factory by the front window. He'd gulped down his weiners fast, but Smith ate much slower. After each bite, Smith chewed thoroughly and then he would talk a little before chomping off another length. Harter wasn't truly listening to what he was saying. For some reason, his mind was more with the onions being spooned on the dogs. Al was at least doing something solid, an action that had an end and left a satisfied customer.

Harter slid around on the wooden bench and managed to tune in on Wayne Smith's voice in time to hear, "So, anyway, they found the gray van about a hundred miles into Ohio, but

216

there's no sign of Schiller's girlfriend. Patty probably hiked up her skirt and hitched a ride from there. Christ, we don't even know her last name. All we can hope is they get good prints and she's been booked before."

"What's it matter?" mumbled Harter.

"Ah, come on. Don't act like you don't care if we pick her up. She pulled a gun on you!"

"She's an accessory at best, if we can even prove that. Hell, she'd say the gun just happened to be in her hand because she was loading it into the van. Our esteemed prosecutor was loud and clear about his legal philosophy last night. He doesn't like to lose cases."

"Don't be such a fucking martyr, Harter. You did all the damn police work, and it took you to Gerald Malcolm. You figured everything out. Sometimes it just doesn't lead to a con-viction. We've all been there before. You know as well as I do that the prosecutor might be right. A jury's more apt to buy the story that Malcolm was only trying to pay Wilton to go away. For all we know, Schiller could have really intended it like that. Maybe Roger Wilton wouldn't disappear and they started argu-ing and Schiller shot him. Anyway, no jury is going to blame Malcolm for how his daughter died, even if he did cover it up. Just let it drop for now. Schiller's girlfriend might give us a whole new angle, if we find her."

"Or she could say she only knew Len Schiller for a week and she never laid eyes on Gerald Malcolm or Roger."

Smith shrugged. "Look. You got Schiller, didn't you? And Malcolm's got to be all torn up inside. Right now, he doesn't know what the prosecutor intends to do, or not do. He and his wife are probably living in dread of what might come out in the papers."

"They lived a lie a long time. I guess they can live in dread awhile." Harter rubbed his index finger around the rim of the empty plate in front of him. "They must have known someone would find out someday."

"You'd think so." Smith stuffed the last of his second hot dog in his mouth and chewed. "Took long enough for the truth to be told, though."

"All the truth except what happened to Nan Wilton. Malcolm claims he had nothing to do with that, either."

"Do you think he did?"

"I don't know."

"Did you ever consider maybe it really was an accident, like Caruthers wrote it off at the time? You know, Caruthers wasn't as bad as you make him out. He could be pretty meticulous. Hell, Harter, you're the one always rattling on about chance. Could just be chance that Nan Wilton was run over a few days after the abortion. She damn well might have been just crossing the street at the wrong moment."

"And they built the pyramids over the pharaohs by chance, too."

"What's that supposed to mean?"

"Something Pete Epstein said last week. Fat chance."

"Sounds like Epstein. So, what did Caruthers have to go on back in Nineteen sixty-seven, anyway? I haven't seen the old report."

Harter noticed that the guy sitting behind Wayne Smith had his head cocked like he was listening to them. "Let's get out of here," he said.

They paid at the cash register, went out the door, and were halfway to the corner before Harter opened up. "Caruthers decided she was hit by a pickup truck."

"Not much help now."

"He thought it might have been blue. Apparently there was a smudge of paint on Nan Wilton's robe."

"A blue pickup." Smith gave a soft laugh as they started across the quiet downtown street.

"What's funny?" asked Harter.

"You remember standing on the corner when you were a kid and watching the traffic? We used to make penny bets about what would come along next, or who could recognize the make and model soonest."

"Or whether it would have out-of-state tags or what color it would be."

"Right."

"I'm sure kids today have more high-tech ways to pass their time. No one even had a TV when I was little."

"Well, Smart Jack, tell me how many blue pickups you remember."

"Got me."

"First off, there weren't as many trucks as today," said Smith as they walked through the parking lot near the police department. "Everyone and his brother wasn't driving around in a pickup with a camper top, not in this town at least. And seems to me nearly all of them were red. Farmers came into Shawnee to shop in red pickups. Remember?"

"Guess so. Except for the Shawnee-Potomac Railroad trucks." Harter saw himself pulling out of Shawnee Community College behind Liz on Tuesday. Saw the blue railroad truck sliding in between them. "They were always blue with a silver insignia like they are now, weren't they?"

Smith nodded as he opened the headquarters door. "State Roads trucks were blue a couple years, but mostly the blue pickups you saw were railroad vehicles." He followed Harter into the building and down the hall toward the detective's office. "Roger Wilton's old man worked for the railroad, didn't he? On the tape from the motel room, Wilton said his father was out of

219

town the week of the abortion, which would also have been about the time of the hit-and-run. Wheat Wilton was supposed to be working a train wreck."

Harter dropped into his chair. "Yeah, he worked for the Shawnee-Potomac." He thought of Matt Curry and Flathead Nash. "So did a couple others I've come across."

"Did you ever get in touch with the railroad and see what you could find out about the wreck and whatever happened that week?"

Harter looked up at Smith and for the first time that day his eyes seemed to have been plugged in. "I know a guy at the Shawnee-Potomac personnel office at the yards. I bet when they went conglomerate and moved the corporate office to Florida, or wherever the hell it is these days, they didn't bother to take all the old records. It's a chance. It's worth a Friday afternoon. You're not such a bad cop, Wayne."

"Thanks for the endorsement. Christ, Harter, I'm nice to women and children, too. In fact, I'll tell you a real secret if you keep it quiet. I've got a bird feeder in my yard, and sometimes I sit by my picture window and watch the birds. I'm a softie. You may not believe this, but one or two of my neighbors even like me."

But Harter's mind was already moving on. "Darrell Phillips killed his wife," he said.

"He's not the first man ever did," said Wayne Smith.

··· 34 ···

Flathead Nash's house looked just as it had five days earlier. The same newspapers rested on the living room rug. The dust on the furniture was no more or less heavy. The picture from Nan Wilton's high school graduation hung on the wall as Nash led Harter and Matt Curry through the front room. On the kitchen table was another plate with egg yolk dried on it. Nash himself wore the same faded flannel shirt, though he had changed his trousers. Once again he spooned instant coffee from the same jar, though he'd soon need to buy a new one.

Harter was playing it all by ear. There were times when the years of experience didn't mean much, didn't teach you anything, didn't add up neatly. In elementary school, they taught you how to check your answers by toting them up the other way, but he couldn't figure out how to double-check this one.

He'd spent the previous afternoon in a room filled with the Shawnee-Potomac Railroad's dead paper. Then, that night from his apartment, he'd called Matt Curry and arranged to pick him up Saturday morning. They'd driven crosstown to Nash's house near the hospital. Near the hospital where Dave and Sally McManaway's baby had been born on Friday. Once this was over, he should go and inspect it.

Flathead Nash brought coffee cups to the table and sat down at the end of it, between Curry and Harter, who sat facing each other. The two old men waited for the cop to talk, and for a second Harter thought maybe he'd made a mistake. What good was it to tell them his suppositions? What good was it to say things that could never be really proven? The old man . . . like Gerald Malcolm, no one was going to put him in jail.

He plowed into it, anyway. First, trying to build up to it logically, Harter began talking about what had happened to Roger. The abortion story was no surprise to either of the old railroaders, but the connection between Len Schiller and Gerald Malcolm was. He tried to explain why Malcolm would probably never be charged with a crime, tried to explain the prosecutor's reasoning, but he didn't even sound convincing to himself. He could read from their faces that Curry and Nash weren't interested in legal manipulations. He'd seen similar expressions before on the faces of men and women who'd grown up in simpler times.

"Goddamn prostituting attorney," said Curry.

"What?" asked Nash.

"That's what Twain wrote one place. Tom and Huck are in a courtroom and one of them complains about the *prostituting* attorney. That's what it bubbles down to."

Harter wasn't in the mood to defend the criminal justice system. He tried to stay calm as he drifted back to December 1967, when Nan had been run down, when the abortion had gone wrong, when the molemen had arrived. He told Nash and Curry about the tape and how Roger had said Wheat was away at a train wreck that week, and how the railroad's records confirmed it. He told them about Caruthers' report on the hit-and-run, and about the blue paint—the blue pickup—the Shawnee-Potomac truck, *maybe*.

He tried to make it clear he was sliding into what-if's, and they seemed to stay with him at every bend. The wreck had been less than fifteen miles from Shawnee. In a narrow cut west of town. Two trains misrouted on the same track. Head-on collision. Two men dead. Main line blocked. They'd worked around the clock for four days to get the rail traffic moving right. They'd brought in a cook and put sleeping cars on the siding so the laborers didn't have to leave the site.

Harter knew enough about working at night, about railroad crews at accident sites—knew enough to realize a person could slip away for a couple of hours. Could drive a truck to town and back. And if there was a dent in the hood or the bumper, well, hell, they were working around wreckage. Maybe the damned thing just rammed into a pile of pulled-up railroad ties. Flathead Nash and Matt Curry knew enough to understand, too.

Harter had learned Wheat Wilton was authorized to drive a railroad truck. He'd come across a file from 1970. Wheat had been involved in a minor accident at a crossing, and there was a statement saying he'd had a spotless driving record until then. His work record in general was clean, though he'd been passed over for promotions more than once.

"The son of a bitch ain't worth a nickel of cat's meat," proclaimed Flathead.

"Remember, I'm just laying out what *could* have happened," Harter cautioned. "We'll never know for sure. We can't make Wheat Wilton say anything. We can't read his mind. No one will ever put him on trial. He'd be declared incompetent as soon as a charge was placed."

Harter took a sip of lukewarm coffee, and the word *incompetent* rolled around in his brain. Darrell Phillips might damn well be incompetent, too.

"Prostituting attorney," Curry mumbled again. "I always felt it was Wheat, but how could I prove it?"

"I can't prove it now," said Harter.

223

"We ought to strangle the bastard," said Flathead.

"Nan told me they were arguing all the time those days," said Matt Curry. "Wheat had hit her. He was calling her from the wreck in the middle of the night and . . ." He twisted his neck and glanced from Harter to Flathead. ". . . and sometimes she wasn't home. The night Roger and her buried the Malcolm girl, Nan heard the phone ring inside, but they were out in the shed and she couldn't get to it in time. Other times, she was with—"

Flathead cut him off. "I want to slug the old asshole."

"You'd wind up in court, and you'd lose," said Harter. "You can't go around hitting people, especially elderly people in the shape Wilton is." He turned back to Curry. "What else did Nan tell you?"

"She'd been looking for a way to get Wheat out of the house so she could do the abortion. She even thought of renting a room somewhere, but then the train wreck happened. Wheat didn't know about the girl being pregnant. Nan kept it from him because it would have just been another reason for Wheat to be hard on Roger. She really protected the boy."

"We ought to push the son of a bitch out his window and let him lay in the middle of the Avenue so the trucks run over him," snarled Flathead.

"It wouldn't bring Nan back," said Curry.

"Well, we ought to at least go down there and let the bastard know we know what he did. Maybe he'd just keel over."

"It won't bring her back, no matter what we do. I always knew it was Wheat. I felt it in my gut. He was turning more jealous each day."

Flathead slammed his fist into the table and the coffee cups jumped. "The cocksucker!"

"What about his daughter—about Nan's daughter?" asked Harter. "Every time I run through what to do, I think of Dorothy. Why put her through the pain at this point? She loves her father."

"And hates her mother," said Flathead.

"She shouldn't hate Nan," said Curry. "If Dorothy knew the whole damn truth, she'd feel different. You're not supposed to hate your mother."

Harter stared across the kitchen table at Matt Curry. "You think Dorothy Merrill would feel better if we spread all this out in front of her? The abortion. Why Nan was crossing the street in the middle of the night. Why you and Wheat couldn't get along. Dorothy already has to deal with her father being a vegetable, and sooner or later she's going to walk in his room one morning and find him dead."

"We ought to help him along," said Flathead.

"None of it is Dorothy Merrill's fault," said Harter.

"Let the bastard live with it," said Curry.

"So we ain't going to do nothing?" Flathead asked.

Harter had an answer, but he waited to see what Matt Curry would come out with.

Slowly, Curry answered. He looked into Flathead's face and he answered. "No, we ain't going to do nothing. Nothing we can do would make a single soul feel an ounce better. Let Wheat sit there frozen, running his sins through his mind."

"If the bastard has any mind left," said Flathead. Some of the fury blew out of his voice in midsentence as what he was saying dawned on him. He reached for his Camels, put one in his mouth, and lit it.

"Sometimes you really hope there's a hell, because even this life isn't bad enough for some people," said Curry.

Straight out, he knew he was wrong. This life could be bad enough. He'd loved Nan, and she'd done a terrible thing, and then she'd been murdered. He'd always known it had been Wheat. But like Harter, he couldn't prove it. Couldn't find the piece that said it all. Many times he'd imagined Wheat sitting in a truck, parked up Egypt Street from his house, waiting for Nan to make her way across. He'd always felt it, but he'd always sealed it in. Hadn't wanted anyone to know all about him and her. Would never do anything to hurt her. Wheat had hurt her enough, all those years. Had hurt him, too.

And then Harter had come back for the third time on Wednesday afternoon. The cop had walked in like he was in charge, like he knew something, like some railroad brass. Curry had listened to his hard questions, and slowly he had decided. The truth had to have less sting than the ghosts.

Thou shalt not commit adultery, his mother would have preached. He could see her. But thou shalt not commit murder, either. Some sins were worse than others. Had to be worse than others. Some sins could not be forgiven. Nan never meant to kill the Malcolm girl, but Wheat had meant to kill Nan. Had planned it out.

He and Wheat, two boys playing along the tracks, among the canalboat ruins. Then they were young men building a shed beside the Wilton place. Then they were courting the same woman. *He loved her.* Then one day they didn't speak any longer.

She was wearing one of those dresses so thin you could see her body move through it, with shiny stockings and high-heel shoes that strapped across her slender ankles. He always remembered her like that. She smelled so clean. Then years later her dress was sliding from her shoulders and she was bending her knee to step free of it. In her lace-edged slip, she crossed the room to him, her arms reaching out. Then one night she was dead.

There wasn't a damn thing he could do to set any of it right.

Old man frozen in place.

... 35 ...

After he watched Matt Curry struggle up the steps to his front door, Harter drove back through Shantytown and out toward the railroad yards. For an instant at the light, he considered turning south and heading to the overlook, but instead he turned the other way on the Avenue and went to headquarters.

He still wasn't certain he'd done the right thing by unloading his conjectures on Curry and Nash. It was too much like weather prognostication in an old almanac, too much guesswork. But somehow he felt better for having done it, and as he'd driven Curry home to Egypt Street, he thought he sensed a relief in the old conductor, too. It was like, right or wrong, there was an end. No one had to live with secrets anymore, though there was still plenty of pain.

Herr, the desk cop, was on the telephone when Harter walked through the door. There was one of those you-won't-believe-this looks on Herr's face, but Harter was all prepared to ignore it. He'd had that feeling himself too many times lately.

"Wait a minute," Herr said to whoever was on the line. So Harter got the message, Herr tilted his head and added, "One of the detectives has just come in. I'll let you talk to him."

Harter pointed down the hall and hurried toward his office.

"Well, what are you going to do about it?" demanded a woman as soon as he picked up the receiver.

"About what?" he asked.

"How many times do I have to explain? I've been calling all day." She was pretty damn mad.

"You haven't explained it to me yet," he answered.

"How are you going to help those people?"

"What people?"

"The ones on the moon."

No wonder Herr had been glad to see him come in. "Back up. I don't know what you're talking about, lady."

"Didn't the other cop tell you? There's people stranded up on the moon."

"How do you know?"

"I saw them. I always look at the full moon with my telescope, just to make sure it's as bright as it should be. Last night was a full moon and I focused in and I saw the people up there. I was so upset I couldn't sleep. No one wants to help them."

"How many people were up there?" Harter asked, a little amazed at his own question.

"At least four. I saw four. Two men and two women. There could have been others on the dark side. They were just standing there, staring back at Earth, staring back at me, with big pleading eyes. They were so worried and lonely. They made me so sad. I don't think they can get back down. They're stuck up there. It's like they're hostages or something."

"You could actually see their faces?"

"Of course. I have a very strong telescope. Why, it cost almost a hundred dollars. They didn't have any food or water with them. They'll die if they can't get home. They were begging me to save them."

"You heard them?"

"Don't be silly. It was more like they were thinking an SOS to me, like they were sending brainwaves. Am I the only one who cares?"

"If they could get up there, I'm sure they can get back. It's like a cat in a tree, isn't it?"

"But they're out of fuel. They were like Noah and his Ark. They were trying to escape the flood, and they ended up on the moon, and now they're out of fuel."

"I don't know what to say. All of our spaceships are busy right now."

"Don't make fun of me, Detective."

"Look, I'm just one of two detectives here. The Shawnee Police Department has enough trouble keeping patrol cars on the road. I don't know how to get to the moon to save anyone."

"A hell of a cop you are!"

Sometimes he was apt to agree with her. "What you need to do is get hold of someone in the federal government. Try the White House."

"I've tried," she said, more belligerent than ever. "It's a weekend. The president's at his ranch. Those people need help now or they'll die up there. There's no oxygen. They can't last long."

"Did you try NASA?"

"NASA?"

"They're in charge of space, aren't they? They're the ones who send astronauts to the moon."

There was a long pause, and then she said, "You're right. I'll call them." He heard a click and soon a dial tone came on.

He dropped the phone into its cradle and pulled out his cigarettes. He had no idea how to rescue people from the moon. He surely wasn't the Wise Old Man of the Mountains. He didn't even know what he was going to have for supper.

He stared at all the papers on his desk, took a second long drag, then snubbed out the cigarette. He thought that if he could clear away all that paper, stuff it in a filing cabinet or something, get it out of his sight, maybe Monday would be different. But he really didn't feel like spending Saturday afternoon moving the junk around.

He glanced over at Caruthers' desk, the one McManaway was using, and he remembered a new baby was in the world. He thought perhaps he'd go up to the hospital and have a look at it, and find McManaway and tell him all that had happened, and then he might drive over the bridge into the West Side and see Liz. If all went well, they might go somewhere on Saturday night and check out the moon and see if the people had gotten down yet.